THE TORTURED WOOD

MALCOLM ROSE

For Elaine Baker for her support
and enthusiasm over the years

With thanks to Hugh Warner

This edition first published in the UK in 2006 by Usborne Publishing Ltd.,
Usborne House, 83-85 Saffron Hill, London EC1N 8RT, England.
www.usborne.com

First published in 2004. Text copyright © Malcolm Rose, 2004.
Cover copyright © Usborne Publishing Ltd., 2006.

A CIP catalogue record for this book is available from the British Library.

ISBN 9780746077436

JFMAMJJAS ND/06

Printed in Great Britain.

1

Dillon shivered. Even before he had turned into the cemetery and taken the trail into Bleakhill Top, he'd been feeling anxious. Now, he was fighting to keep fear at bay. He wished he'd kept to the roads. It was much spookier in the wood than he'd expected. Winter had stripped the leaves from the trees, leaving dark skeletons that swayed and creaked uncannily in the gloom. He could hear water gushing somewhere nearby, but strangely he could not see any streams. Weaving between the stark trees, the narrow footpath was not well marked. Last year's brambles overhung it and grasped at his spotless school trousers. Tree roots had burst through the soil and crossed the track like the rungs of a ladder. On his right, the ground sloped steeply down to the floor of the valley.

It was his first day at a new school and he was beginning to think that the older students who had directed him through the wood had played a trick on him. His family had moved just before Christmas, so Dillon was having to start school partway through the year and he wasn't looking forward to it.

He peered around suspiciously. There was nothing but trees. If this path really was a short cut, he thought, some of the other students would be trampling along it. There'd be the sounds of kids mucking about, shouting, throwing sticks. But it was eerily quiet. Dillon had memorized the map, though, and he knew he was going in the right direction so he carried on warily.

The sun was still lurking behind the ridge on his left, making the clouds glow pink, not yet throwing much light and warmth into the valley of Eastbridge at the edge of the wild moors. Wisps of morning mist snaked through the wood like lost souls. There was a noise like a hiss, followed by a loud squawk. Dillon gasped, unsure where it had come from, but instinctively he looked up. A dark form fell heavily from one of the bare branches and landed with a thud behind him. Feathers drifted down towards him like strips of black paper.

Brushing a piece of the ghoulish confetti from the shoulder of his thick coat, Dillon turned round and stared at the ground. A blackbird lay dead on the path. Dillon shuddered. A sad sigh came out of his mouth as a miniature cloud. He looked up again but saw nothing, no sign of movement in the branches.

THE TORTURED WOOD

He tried to tell himself that the bird's fate was probably natural but, even if he was right, it wasn't a good omen. At least the blackbird's body hadn't hit him. That would have been gross.

Dillon didn't know why but this particular tree made his skin crawl. It was stark and angular, large enough to be menacing, yet also somehow sad. Dillon wouldn't have been surprised to hear that, at some point in its history, people had been hanged from its twisted branches. Trembling, Dillon moved out from underneath the lime tree and continued to trudge through the wood in the direction of the school.

Almost at once he halted and let out another gasp, his heart thudding. Down in the wood to the right of the path there was a large man standing totally still, staring furiously up at him. Dillon wasn't sure whether to run or shout for help. Hesitating before he did either, he peered again through the shadows at the startling figure and realized that he'd been tricked again. He was looking at a woodcarving. Luckily, he'd caught on before making a complete fool of himself. The statue of the angry man had been cut from the trunk of a dead oak. There was even a carved dog sitting at his heel. The pet terrier seemed just as vicious as the man himself. Both of them looked so lifelike that Dillon expected them to stride into the distance, but their feet were rooted in the ground.

Relieved, Dillon managed a wry smile as his heart rate slowed. This was probably why the older boys had sent him through the wood. They'd thought he would be scared by the wooden sculpture. Well, they were right. Dillon was expecting them to jump out from behind tree trunks and have a good laugh at his expense but they didn't. He was still alone. Trying to avoid tripping on the bulging roots, he hurried along as quickly as he could. On his first day he didn't want to be late.

He was ready for the second carving. He wasn't frightened this time, but he was fascinated. On the flatter ground to his left, a dead tree was leaning towards the track as if it had been frozen in the act of falling. On the underside of the hefty trunk, another man had been etched. His face was contorted with pain to make it look as if the weight of the tree were crushing him. Dillon decided that the artist who had chiselled this sculpture must be both talented and mad. He didn't know whether he admired the carver's skill or was sickened by the bizarre snapshot of a terrible accident. Probably both.

The face of the man under the falling tree had been fashioned carefully to be grotesque yet realistic. It was twisted sideways so that walkers could get a good view from the track. One of the man's cheeks, a shoulder and a leg melded with the wood so it appeared that the trunk was already crushing him. His agony was perfectly captured but it didn't invite sympathy. Dillon felt that the artist had enjoyed the man's despair.

Forgetting the time, Dillon left the path and walked towards the cruel sculpture. He didn't know how an image could be so repulsive and so captivating at the same time. Slowly, he put out his hand to touch that tortured face, to feel the painstaking detail. He could almost believe that the face would be warm and soft like real flesh but it felt freezing to his fingertips. And, of course, it was rigid. Nothing at all like skin. Dillon didn't know whether to feel relieved or disappointed.

He turned to walk away, intending to scurry along to school, when he lost his footing on the slippery layer of decomposing leaves. His hand slammed down to break his fall. He cried out in surprise and shock. Something solid and sharp had torn into his thumb and his blood was oozing onto the ground.

2

Shocked, Dillon watched the deep red drops from his thumb splash onto the soggy brown leaves and disappear. The decaying vegetation lapped up his blood as if it needed the liquid to revive the trees. The cut didn't hurt, but Dillon felt a throbbing in his thumb. He didn't have anything to stem the bleeding, and he certainly didn't want to spoil his new uniform any further. Anyway, the wound wasn't too serious and the trickling blood had already cleaned it. Not knowing anything better to do, he shoved his thumb into his mouth.

Cautiously, with his other hand, he cleared away some of the leaves, trying to find out what had pierced his flesh. It didn't take long to unearth a strip of metal and slide it out of the mud. It was the blade of a chisel. Checking again that no one was around, Dillon examined his find. The tool's soiled wooden handle was ancient. If it had ever been painted or treated, it had long since lost its coating. But it hadn't cracked or rotted. Amazingly, there was no sign of rust on the blade. It looked incredibly sharp and keen, perfect for slicing through bark and wood. And skin. Dillon guessed that he was holding the woodcarver's chisel, the one that had shaped such anger and suffering in the two sculptures. But it wasn't the tool's fault. It was just a thing, lifeless in his palm. It could sculpt only what was in its owner's warped mind.

THE TORTURED WOOD

There was an unnerving scratching noise somewhere behind him, maybe a bird or a rat among the dead leaves and twigs. Dillon put the dirty chisel carefully into his backpack and scrambled to his feet. Examining his thumb, he was pleased to see that the cut had stopped bleeding. He returned to the path and then dashed through the rest of the deserted wood towards Eastbridge High School.

At morning break, the school playground was the opposite of Bleakhill Top: tarmac, brick, noise and swarming students. For Dillon, not yet belonging to any of the rowdy groups, the yard held a threat of an entirely different sort. He felt like a lone fox among a pack of hounds. He was exaggerating, of course. They weren't baying for his blood. Many of them simply ignored him. Mostly, they gazed at him and, not recognizing him, frowned and turned away. Dillon thought that a few looked guilty as they gave him the cold shoulder. A smaller boy knocked his arm as he ran to catch a rugby ball. Only Dillon offered an apology.

A few seconds later, someone crashed into him from behind. This time, it wasn't an accident. Dillon felt his backpack being dragged from his back. He spun round to see three grinning Year 9 boys. The student holding his bag was the one who'd directed him through Bleakhill Top.

"Enjoy your walk to school?" said the boy in a mocking tone.

"It was okay," Dillon replied casually. "Nothing special."

For a moment the lad looked surprised, then he decided to call Dillon's bluff. "If it was okay, you can go that way every day." He knelt down and undid Dillon's backpack. "What have we got in here?" His two mates squatted either side of him.

"Not a lot." Dillon knew what was happening, of course. As the new boy, he was being tested. If he stood there, said nothing, and took it all, he'd be branded as weak, a target for the bullies. If he shouted for the teacher on duty, the boys would make his life hell for ever after. If he objected and thumped or kicked the nearest pupil, they might leave him alone, might rate him, but they'd probably thump or kick him back. Then they'd discover that he didn't really have the heart for fighting. Not sure what was best to do, Dillon attempted to look cool, as if he didn't care what they did. He tried to banish all visible traces of anxiety from his face and instead wore an expression of contempt for the boys. Inside, though, he was tense and angry. This wouldn't have happened at his old school in Ipswich. There, he had friends – good friends – and respect. Here, in Eastbridge, he had nothing.

Most of the other kids pretended that they hadn't seen what was happening. A few looked on, probably too scared to do anything about it.

With a look of both triumph and shock on

his face, one of the boys pulled the muddy chisel from Dillon's backpack. He was about to lay into Dillon when a teacher appeared.

Mr. Quillen looked like a skeleton with papery skin stretched over its bones. He was tall, and his wispy white hair blew around chaotically in the wind. The cold air gave him a red nose but the rest of his skin was pale like a ghost's. Head angled downwards, he looked at Dillon severely over his small spectacles. "Are you the new boy?"

"Dillon Carthy."

The teacher gazed at the three students squatting around Dillon's backpack. "What's this?" he asked, although he'd already figured it out for himself. "Luke?"

The Year 9 student looked down at the old chisel in his hand and replied, "It's not mine. It's his." He nodded towards Dillon.

"If it's not yours," Mr. Quillen said, "why have you got it?"

"We were just…" Luke ran out of explanation.

"You were harassing a new boy. Not for the first time." The teacher shook his head, inhaled deeply and then let the breath go noisily. "Luke, Simon and Cliff. I'll see you in my room at twelve thirty. Now give Dillon his bag back. And give me that thing." Once the three boys had walked away, muttering their grievances, Mr. Quillen peered at the dirty chisel. This time he inspected it through the lenses of his glasses. He seemed horrified. Turning to Dillon, he said, "This is just as bad as carrying a knife. You'll go to the Deputy Head and explain yourself. Right now."

First, Dillon attempted to defend himself. "I didn't mean to bring it in. I just found it on the way to school – the wood."

"In the wood?" the teacher exclaimed in disbelief. "No one goes into the wood."

"I was told it was a short cut."

"Who told you?"

Dillon shrugged. Not knowing why he was protecting Luke, he replied, "Just some boys."

"And that's where you picked this up?" Mr. Quillen looked down at the chisel, suspicion in his eyes. He clasped it carefully between forefinger and thumb, like a police officer might hold a murder weapon to avoid smearing it with fingerprints.

"Yes."

"Even so…" Mr. Quillen made a tutting noise. "I don't suppose you know Miss Wright's office so I'll take you." He got a better grip on the chisel and winced as if it were burning into the flesh of his fingers. "You'll see me at the end of the day in the Arts Faculty to get this back and you won't bring it into school ever again. Understand?"

"Yes, Sir."

"If it was up to me…" Opening a door into one of the school corridors, he was distracted by another member of staff who exchanged a few words with him. He didn't finish his sentence.

THE TORTURED WOOD

Dillon wasn't a natural troublemaker. As he was marched down the corridor, he couldn't believe that things were moving so fast in the wrong direction. His first day at the school was turning out to be far worse than he'd imagined. And it was all because of those boys, Bleakhill Top and the horrific carvings. If he hadn't discovered the chisel, he wouldn't be in this mess. Yet he wasn't blaming the chisel. He was the one who'd decided to pick it up and put it in his bag. And that was because his instinct told him it was right that he'd found it, as if it had always meant to be his.

3

Moments later, Dillon found himself standing in front of the Deputy Head, staring at the floor, explaining again how he happened to have a sharp tool in his bag.

"So," she said when she'd heard him out, "it isn't a weapon?"

Dillon looked aghast. "No, Miss."

"And you didn't bring it in case you got a bit of aggro on your first day?"

"No."

"All right. I believe you. It's school policy that everyone gets a chance to prove themselves. We only come down hard on people if they snub that chance so, this time, I'm giving you the benefit of the doubt. I won't put you on a yellow card. It's your first day after all." She sat up straight and stared at Dillon. "Never bring it – or anything like it – back into school. Otherwise...deep trouble."

Dillon nodded.

"Right. You can expect random checks in the next week or so but, otherwise, the matter's closed." She sat back behind her desk without releasing him from her gaze. "Before you go, you'd better hear something about Bleakhill Top, especially being new to the area. It's best coming from me because your new colleagues out there might tell you all sorts."

"Oh?"

Miss Wright said, "I live down the road in Sheffield but I know the people round here steer clear of it. The council says it's unsafe – falling trees and that sort of thing. At least a couple of people have been injured there, that's for sure. More, I think. I've also heard people say there was a fight there once, but..." She shrugged. "Even if there's a lot of imagination in these stories, they're good reasons to avoid it, don't you think?"

Dutifully, Dillon answered, "Yes." He paused before asking, "I was just thinking... There's some carvings. Do you know who did them?"

The Deputy Head glanced out of the window before looking back, once more gazing into Dillon's eyes. "I've heard about these wood sculptures, but I haven't seen them. No doubt they're behind a lot of the more outlandish stories. And they've caused quite a bit of grief. You're not thinking of doing your own carvings, are you? Is that what the chisel's about?"

Dillon hadn't thought of it until Miss Wright mentioned it. "No."

"Good. I can't regulate what you do when you're well away from the school but I can advise. I suggest that you keep out. It's dangerous. Okay?"

"Yes, Miss."

"Right." She let out a long breath and then changed the subject. "It's not easy to integrate into a new school in the middle of the year, is it?"

"It's all right…" But Dillon's tone and expression gave him away.

Miss Wright looked down at some papers on her desk. "Your last school tells me you play a mean piano."

"Keyboard and guitar as well," Dillon stressed. They had much more street cred than piano. "I was in a band."

"We'll have to make the most of you. I'll talk to the music teacher. And," she added, "I gather you haven't been given a mentor yet, another Year 8 boy.

Do you know what I mean?"

Dillon nodded again.

"Well, I'm sorry. It should've been done. That's school policy as well. Teachers are run off their feet at the start of term. So, I'll choose someone we can both trust and he'll help you settle in."

Dillon wasn't convinced that he liked the sound of a mentor but he replied, "Thank you."

"I'll assign someone this afternoon and make sure he sees you before going-home time. Is that a deal?"

"Yes. Thanks."

Lessons over for the day, Dillon went in search of Mr. Quillen in the big art room at the end of the corridor. The place was awash with artwork. Paintings, sketches, photographs and computer-generated images on the walls, models and pottery on the benches. There were no woodcarvings as far as Dillon could see. Some of the pieces were joyful, some abstract, some bizarre. And some expressed horror, like the small clay head cleaved open by an embedded hatchet. These made Dillon wince, but guessed they were supposed to and that's why they were on display. The budding artists had not always been successful but their intentions were clear every time.

Silently and stealthily, Mr. Quillen walked up to him like some creepy, leggy insect. "Dillon Carthy," he said, showing off the fact that he'd memorized the name. "That chisel's safely locked away in my cupboard. Before I get it, though, let me say this: if it was up to me, I'd get rid of it. Wrap the blade in newspaper and bin the thing. Don't have anything to do with it. Don't get involved."

Dillon was puzzled and he felt a shiver inside. He wasn't sure what the art teacher meant. It was almost as if Mr. Quillen knew more about the chisel than he was willing to admit. Dillon didn't query it, though.

He just wanted to get out as quickly as possible. Saying exactly what the teacher wanted to hear, he replied, "Yes, Sir."

"And don't go back into Bleakhill Top and dump it there. It's not safe, as I think you've been told. Besides, it's not a good idea to leave such a thing lying about."

"No, I won't."

Suddenly, Mr. Quillen gripped him tightly around the wrist. "We're agreed on that, are we?"

Dillon looked down at the long fingers clutching him. They were gnarled like the bark of a tree. Unsettled, he nodded.

"Sure?"

"Yes," Dillon replied, his voice breaking.

"Okay."

Dillon let out a breath when the art teacher released his arm.

Mr. Quillen went to a large cupboard and yanked open the door. Inside, it was layered with shelves.

When he took the chisel, he shuddered as if a cockroach were scuttling across his palm.

Before the teacher shut the cupboard door, Dillon saw lots of equipment and some more artwork. Among it, he thought he caught sight of a face – Mr. Quillen's unmistakable face – carved cleverly in a small section of a branch.

"Here," Mr. Quillen said, quickly returning the chisel as if he didn't want to hold it for a second longer than necessary. "Remember what I've said – what we've agreed. Believe me, you don't want to see what it can do."

In Dillon's hand, the tool felt snug and warm. Slipping it back into his backpack, he was delighted to escape from the weird teacher.

Outside, it was chilly and damp, but not quite frosty. The snow that had fallen lightly on the three days following Christmas had melted away by New Year's Day. Dillon guessed that it would be nowhere near as bleak in Ipswich.

By the school gates, a large boy yelled at him. "Hey! You."

Dillon groaned inwardly. Not *another* local lad intent on giving him a hard time... Dillon wasn't going to wait to find out. He took off down the road.

Behind him, the voice shouted, "Just a minute! Stop!"

Dillon charged as fast as he could with his backpack clunking against him. He barged past two girls who called after him, "Watch it, stupid!"

Glancing over his shoulder, Dillon saw that the boy was sprinting and would soon catch him up. Panting, Dillon knew one certain way to escape. He rounded the corner by the newsagent's and, instead of carrying on along the pavement, he veered up the overgrown footpath that led to Bleakhill Top. No one would follow him there. The only problem was that the sun was setting. Night already had the wood in its eerie grip.

4

At first, Dillon's daylight eyes could not cope with the gloom in the wood. He stumbled forward blindly, away from one danger, into another. The trees on either side of the track leaned in towards each other like sinister couples holding hands. Underneath them, Dillon felt small and hemmed in. He felt as though the wooden arms were reaching out to throttle him. He imagined the branches coiling round him like a boa constrictor, slowly squeezing life from him. He told himself not to be silly but, as the darkening wood stirred eerily, it wasn't easy. Unseen crows scrabbled among the branches, rats scratched around in the undergrowth, and a solitary owl hooted. All of the noise of the normal world – cars and kids – was blocked by the screen of trees. He could have been on a different planet, the sole human being in an unfamiliar and hostile terrain.

Without warning, Dillon felt a stinging sensation across his cheek, as if someone had slashed at him with the sharp point of a knife. He let out a pained, "Ouch." At the same time, he jolted away and his hand darted to his face. But there was no one in the wood with him. His eyes adjusting to the dark, he saw the holly that had ripped his skin.

Breathlessly, he went on as quickly as he could, hoping to emerge on the opposite side of the copse into the friendly orange glow of streetlamps before complete blackness engulfed Bleakhill Top. Near the two carvings, though, the path was treacherously slippery, so he had to slow down. If he lost his footing again, he could fall to his left and tumble all the way down the hill – unless he hit a tree or a rock first. Either way, he wouldn't stand a chance.

Peering around as he went, he noticed that quite a few trees had keeled over as if their roots did not have a firm foundation. Like the risen dead, some were trying to sprout again, the saplings growing at crazy angles from toppled trunks. Plainly, the Deputy Head and Mr. Quillen were right about the wood being risky because of falling trees. Dillon also spotted a third carving. In the dusk, he wasn't sure what it portrayed, but he hoped that it wasn't as disturbing as the other two. It showed a human figure, perhaps with angel's wings, and that was all he could see. He didn't dare to scramble down the bank to get a better look at it.

For a moment he hesitated by the lime tree where the blackbird had died but then he moved on with a jolt, hurrying past it. Head bowed, he made for the cemetery on the main road, open air and safety. From the burial ground, a single row of modest houses skirted the northern edge of the wood. To the west, there was nothing but the rugged moorland of the Peak District. By day, it looked both desolate and attractive. In this light, it was a wild and unwelcoming landscape. Dillon dreaded to think what might be out there. Quickly, he headed for home.

It was Monday, 6th January and a few of the houses were still decorated with lights. A twinkling star, a chubby Santa Claus, glistening icicles dangling from guttering. They'd been bright and cheerful over Christmas but now they looked sad and neglected, like leftovers. Christmas in Dillon's new house had been strange. His mum and dad had perched the Christmas tree on an upturned cardboard box. Their usual decorations had been lost in the move. Dillon's dad had bought a cheap and cheerful set of coloured lights for the front window and that was about it.

When Dillon got home, he had to explain the scratch on his face and the cut on his thumb without telling his parents about Bleakhill Top. They wouldn't have approved of him going into a dangerous wood on his own, so it would have to remain his secret. He also kept quiet about getting into trouble over the chisel. He didn't try to hide the difficulty of fitting in, though. He couldn't disguise the fact that he didn't feel welcome or accepted.

"I know what it's like," Mr. Carthy said to him over dinner. "They're a proud lot round here and maybe they think they don't need new people. But it's not such a big deal, settling in. I'm having to do it with my new job. As soon as you build up a bit of trust, you'll make friends. Real good friends. Just don't be shy. You've got to work at it, and be patient."

His mum said, "I know it's tough, love, that you're getting hassled at school but I guess it's to be expected with you being the new boy. It'd be the same for someone moving from Eastbridge to Ipswich, I'm sure. And it won't last long. Soon, you won't be new any more. They'll get used to you and you to them."

"That's right," his dad added. "And until everything settles down, it's a matter of asserting yourself, and not standing for any nonsense."

"Easier said than done."

His mum smiled sympathetically. "Believe me, love, you're much tougher than you think."

Maybe he was. His parents had always supported him, but they also believed that he'd never learn if they solved all of his problems, so they encouraged him to use his own initiative. Since moving, most of their time and energy had gone into the new house, so Dillon had been forced to stand on his own two feet even more than usual.

Mrs. Carthy turned to her husband, going back yet again to the topic of their new home. She seemed to talk about little else. "We're going to have to get something done about the drive, you know. It's more pothole than drive. When the hard frosts come, it'll crack up completely. The neighbours don't seem that friendly but I'll ask them if they know anyone who can sort it out."

"Yeah. Why not?" Dillon's dad replied. "And you could ask around at school, Dillon."

"What?"

Mr. Carthy made a playful tutting noise. "You weren't listening."

"I was thinking about school." He was lying. He was thinking about Bleakhill Top and its carvings. As soon as the meal was over, Dillon was going to examine the chisel again.

His dad said, "And I was trying to give you something to talk to the other pupils about. One of them might have a dad who fixes drives." Then he tucked into his sausage.

Dillon had no intention of taking up his dad's

dumb suggestion on how to start a conversation. Alone in his bedroom, he extracted the chisel from his bag and held it in his hand. The wood was just rough enough to provide a good grip, not so coarse that it scuffed his skin. Its shape moulded to his fist beautifully, uncannily, as if it had been made to measure. He crept along to the bathroom, washed away the mud from the tool and then dried it carefully on some tissues. The end of the handle was jagged and compacted where it had been hit repeatedly with a mallet, but it had stood up well to the punishment. There wasn't a patch of corrosion on the blade. The curved steel tip, made for gouging out wood, was shiny, sharp and ready. It was such a pity to throw it out.

Dillon's spine tingled unpleasantly as he sat on his bed and looked closely at the handle. Someone had scratched a couple of letters into it where the steel emerged from the wood. They were small and worn but clearly recognizable. The chisel was inscribed with the initials *DC*. Dillon swallowed hard. It had to be a coincidence. There were probably lots of people who shared his initials. The tool could belong to any of them. Even so, those small scratched letters were really spooky.

He was beginning to understand Mr. Quillen's suspicion of the chisel. Dillon could not believe that the art teacher would be so wary – even scared – without good reason. Although Dillon felt drawn to the chisel, he was also troubled by it. Remembering Mr. Quillen's heartfelt advice, Dillon went quietly downstairs to the recycling bin and took a few newspaper pages. He wrapped the paper around the blade several times to protect prying fingers from its sharpness. Nipping outside while his mum and dad were watching TV, he opened the wheelie bin, paused, sighed and finally dropped the veiled tool on top of all of the other rubbish. He went back to his room feeling strangely empty.

* * *

The next morning, the boy who had chased Dillon after school collared him in the playground. Taking refuge in the wood yesterday had delayed rather than called off the confrontation. "You'll get us into right trouble, you will," the lad said.

"Pardon?" Dillon didn't understand.

The boy, big for Year 8, stood there with a sidekick each side of him. Dillon had seen bullies at work and he knew that they never acted alone. A bully always wanted his mates to watch – and admire. Either that or it took several of them to egg each other on.

Dillon looked around, hoping a teacher would be on duty nearby, but it was too much to expect to be rescued by Mr. Quillen again. He took a deep breath to steel himself.

"You are Dillon Carthy, aren't you?"

"Yes."

"Ainsley," the boy said, introducing himself. "I were supposed to see you yesterday. I've been assigned to you. I've to help you find your feet."

"Oh." Dillon felt as if he'd just shaken off a dreadful headache, but outwardly he tried to appear indifferent. "You don't have to." He thought it was humiliating to be allocated a friend – as if these things could be dictated – and Ainsley didn't look overjoyed with his task.

Ainsley shrugged. "I've been told to."

"You don't really want to be with me." Dillon made it sound halfway between a question and a statement.

"I don't want Spanish homework either, but I still do it," Ainsley replied bluntly and honestly but without hostility. "Treat you like a brother, Miss Wright said. Which means giving you a right good thumping at every opportunity." Along with his friends, he laughed. "No, I think the idea's for me to tell you who to keep clear of, and try to get you in with my mates."

Dillon hesitated. He wanted real friends. He didn't want to hang out with boys who did it as a duty. He suspected, though, that Ainsley's offer was his best bet till he felt comfortable and confident in his new surroundings.

Detecting Dillon's uncertainty, Ainsley said, "Come on. We're on us way to see who's been picked for the rugby team."

"Rugby?" Dillon tried to keep his groan inaudible. Just because he was a boy, everyone expected him to be interested in sport, but he wasn't. In some people's eyes, that made him a wimp.

"Yeah," Ainsley replied. "It's the thing around here. Let's face it, if you go for soccer, you've got to support Sheffield Wednesday or Barnsley." He shrugged, his point made.

Dillon followed them to the notice board where Simon, Luke and Cliff were already celebrating their selection. They turned towards Ainsley, about to greet a fellow team member, when they caught sight of Dillon in tow.

"Hey!" Luke exclaimed. "We got red cards from Quillen because of you."

"Oh?" Dillon answered, feeling braver now that he was with Ainsley and his friends. "Not because of what you were doing?"

"No way."

As soon as the three of them had retreated, Ainsley glanced at Dillon with a smile. "First lesson," he said. "Luke, Cliff and Simon. Good rugby players but best kicked into touch. Especially Cliff. He's had it rough, but that were a year ago. Keep your distance, if I was you."

Dillon nodded. He didn't really need telling.

"You should do a trial for the team. You looked nifty on your feet yesterday."

"I don't think so," Dillon muttered. There wasn't a scrap of meat on him. He was reasonably fast because he wasn't carrying any weight but, if he got tackled, he'd come to a bone-shuddering dead stop. Contact sports weren't his strength.

Ainsley looked him up and down. "Maybe not," he said. "Why did you run, anyway?"

Dillon shrugged. "I was late for something."

"You ran into Bleakhill Top. Hasn't anyone told you about that?"

"Yes."

"But you still went in?"

"Yes."

"Brave or stupid, then. Council used to put up barriers and keep-out notices but some kids always tore them down. They don't bother any more. No one goes in anyway."

"Why not?" Dillon asked.

"I thought someone told you. Miss Wright and Quillen."

"They didn't tell me why exactly."

Ainsley smiled faintly and knowingly as if he understood why teachers would not want to reveal all about Bleakhill Top. In a matter-of-fact voice, he said, "It's haunted."

5

"Haunted?" Dillon replied doubtfully. "Do you really believe that?"

"Of course." Ainsley leaned towards him and lowered his voice. "I wouldn't go in. They say a woman were beaten to death and buried in there. Her body's never been found but they say it makes the ground shift. Restless spirit and stuff. That's why trees fall over."

"Oh." Dillon didn't know what to say. He wasn't sure if he believed in ghosts, particularly ones that pushed trees over.

Ainsley pointed to the fine red line on Dillon's right cheek and asked, "Did she scratch you with her nails?"

"No. It was a bush."

Ignoring Dillon's unexciting explanation, Ainsley whispered, "If you're right quiet, you can hear her crying, they say. Did you hear anything?"

Dillon shrugged. "Nothing like that. There was running water. That's all."

Ainsley glanced significantly at his friends. "And did you see a river?"

"No."

"That's because there isn't one," Ainsley replied. He leaned even closer and said, "You heard her that was murdered. She were crying."

If it hadn't been for Ainsley's sincere face, Dillon would have thought that he was being wound up. He shivered inwardly but still didn't believe

Ainsley's explanation of the weird noise. "I'll tell you what I did see."

"What's that?"

"Woodcarvings. You know. Tree stumps shaped with a chisel."

Ainsley pulled back sharply and looked towards the distant playing field.

"They're a bit...nasty," Dillon added. "Good, clever, but nasty."

"We don't talk about them."

"Why not?"

Ainsley muttered, "We just don't."

"Well, do you know who did them?"

Ainsley shook his head. "No one really knows."

Dillon looked into his face, suspecting that he was lying, but asked no more.

On the way home, Dillon and Ainsley both glanced up at the path leading to Bleakhill Top yet said nothing and continued along the pavement, beyond the reach of any bad spirits.

But they weren't beyond the reach of the crowd of kids outside the newsagent's. Some were kicking an empty can around, others were having a crafty smoke. On seeing Dillon, they stopped and stared. Once Dillon and Ainsley had gone past, the can flew over Dillon's shoulder, narrowly missing his head. It was followed by shouted insults.

"Ignore it," said Ainsley.

"I guess that's why they told you to walk home with me?"

"Part of the way. You live past my place."

"But is that why?"

Ainsley shrugged. "Suppose so. They wanted me to make sure you didn't go back into the wood as well."

"Thought so." Ainsley was Dillon's protection from Cliff, Luke, Simon and maybe others. Ill at ease, Dillon waited for a few seconds before asking, "Why have they got it in for me?"

Pointing across the road, Ainsley said, "See that white van, parked over there?"

"Yeah."

"It belongs to a gardener. Pete. He does old folk and posh people. I know him, I know almost everyone around here and they know me. See what it says on the back?"

Across the rear doors was written, BORN TO BE AN EASTBRIDGER.

Ainsley smiled. "That's why they get at you. It's a small place, not like Sheffield. They don't take kindly to strangers. They're slow to take anything new on board. That's all."

Dillon cursed his mum and dad for bringing him to this awful town, for taking him away from friends and security. "There's nothing wrong with me, then. It's them."

"You've got a point there. But it's just the way things are in Eastbridge."

Along the lane, the streetlamps were just coming

on. All of the showy Christmas lights had disappeared from the houses and gardens. Everything had returned abruptly to normal. Of course, none of it was really normal to Dillon.

Once Ainsley had turned off for his own house, Dillon slogged uphill towards home. As he went, he replayed what Ainsley had said about the woodcarvings. He hadn't said, "No, I don't know who did the carving." He'd said, "No one really knows." That meant he'd got a good idea who the artist was but he couldn't be certain and he wasn't going to talk about it.

Dillon was going to have to investigate it on his own, but he had already thrown away the best piece of evidence that linked him to the unknown artist.

On the path up to his front door, Dillon came to a halt. He couldn't walk past the wheelie bin without peering inside. Yes, it was still there, wrapped in yesterday's news, on top of a black bin bag. He reached down, paused, withdrew his hand and then, making up his mind, grabbed the chisel, plucked it out and slipped it into his backpack.

Until his dad came home from work, Dillon played the keyboards. His mum did her best to lift his quiet mournful tunes with a bright hum but even her silvery voice didn't manage to steer him into more upbeat territory.

It was the usual routine when Mr. Carthy got home. In turn, they each reported on their day. Since the move, Dillon's day had slipped down the pecking order.

"I put the lights away and chucked the tree out," said his mum.

"Good."

"We were a day late but, under the circumstances, we'll probably be let off. It was only a few hours overdue."

"Let off what?" Dillon asked.

"They say you get bad luck if you leave decorations up after the twelfth day of Christmas," his dad answered. "But it's superstitious nonsense."

Dillon nodded and frowned at the same time.

"Anyway," Mr. Carthy continued, "how was school? No more bother from the kids?"

"I've got a friend," Dillon replied. "Ainsley." Reporting the high and leaving aside the lows, he didn't tell his parents that this was a friend who had been bribed with merit points to take care of him.

"Excellent," his dad said, relieved that he did not have to worry any more about his son.

And that was it. It would be a while before the conversation turned to his lessons, teachers and homework.

After Mr. Carthy had described every last detail of his working day, he looked across the table at his wife. "What else did you do today?"

"Oh, you know. Fixing things up, rearranging, cleaning, cooking, assembling furniture. So, nothing much. I'm just a plumber, electrician, cook, cleaner and carpenter."

"Yeah, but you don't do tarmac, unfortunately."

"No," she replied, "and the neighbours don't know anyone who'll do it at a good price, either. Not that they seemed particularly keen to help out."

"Pity." Mr. Carthy hesitated before adding, "You need a break. How about going out for a drink tonight?"

While his mum and dad talked about the house, going through it room by room, Dillon was quiet, drifting. His mind was occupied with ghosts, murder, the restless wood, a tortured artist and bad luck. If, at the end of the meal, his mum had asked him what he'd just eaten, he wouldn't have known. But he did know that he had to find out more about the mysterious Bleakhill Top. Putting down his spoon, he said, "While you're out, I'm going online. Is that okay?"

His dad breathed in noisily as if it pained him to

agree. "I suppose so. But not for too long. We're not having a big telephone bill on top of everything else."

In less than a second, an online search gave him the website address of *The Eastbridge Journal*. Dillon didn't want to browse the newspaper's archive because he didn't know any dates. Instead he entered *Bleakhill Top carving murder* into the website's search engine. No articles matched all four words. Nothing matched the whole of *Bleakhill Top carving*, *Bleakhill Top ghost* or *Bleakhill Top fight* either. Instead, he retrieved all of the articles that appeared under *Bleakhill Top*.

Scrolling through the headlines, none caught his eye until two of them made his blood run cold. *Tragic Accident in Bleakhill Top* and *Second Death in Bleakhill Top*.

6

His skin crawling, Dillon stared at the screen, reading the first article. Apparently, a year ago, the town councillors had been made aware of vandalism taking place in Bleakhill Top. The report didn't say what harm had been done in the wood but, when a council inspector had gone there to assess the damage, he was so seriously injured by a falling tree that he died from his injuries a few hours later in hospital.

Dillon could not get to the end of the brief piece without seeing that awful carving in his mind. The dreadful image now in his brain was as clear as the real thing in the wood – the tree falling, the unbearable pressure of its weight crushing the inspector's face, shoulder and leg, the harrowing expression of pain, and the artist's obvious delight in sculpting the detail. Dillon shivered. Perhaps the carver was cruel as well as mad.

The second article, published a couple of months later, reported on the attempt to deal with the vandalism. Again it had ended in failure and disaster. This time, there was an accident that had nothing to do with the trees. As soon as the council workers started the job, one of them had been struck by lightning.

A few minutes after James Aykroyd went into Bleakhill Top, a violent storm hit the area. Local resident Mrs. Alice Burkinshaw told The Eastbridge Journal: *"The van pulled up outside and three of them went off into Bleakhill Top. In next to no time, everything went really dark and then there was this lightning. I've never seen anything like it. You could hear it crackle. And the thunder nearly shook the house down. The storm was right on top of us."*

The other two workmen were brothers. Stuart and Paul Oxley suffered serious but not fatal burns. James Aykroyd was killed instantly. He was born in Eastbridge and had always lived in the town. His family is well known locally. He leaves a wife and son.

Following Mr. Aykroyd's death, the second fatality connected with Bleakhill Top, the council has decided that the wood should be declared out of bounds. A spokesman commented: *"It's highly unlikely that any more of our operatives will be asked to work in*

Bleakhill Top and even less likely that any of them would volunteer."

Dillon was relieved that the woodland artist hadn't shown him an image of James Aykroyd's accident. The thought of being blasted by lightning was bad enough without seeing a sculpture of it as well.

Logging off, Dillon felt that he had a better grasp of events in Bleakhill Top but he didn't have a complete picture. He was still puzzled. The attempt to remove the damage had failed, so whatever it was should still be there. But Dillon hadn't seen any graffiti, broken benches, abandoned shopping trolleys, burned-out cars. Nothing. So what was this vandalism that the council had been desperate to inspect and then remove?

He reasoned that there was no mention of the wood sculptures in *The Eastbridge Journal* because they would have been carved after the deaths. The articles could not tell him who had recreated the image of that first tragic accident – and why. Had the artist actually seen the death or merely imagined it after reading the newspaper? Dillon presumed that, to make such a realistic figure, the woodcarver must have witnessed the accident. If so, why had the sculptor been in the wood at the time?

There was nothing on the website about a ghost, a fight or a woman's murder. Perhaps they were just rumours, made up deliberately as a ploy to keep people away. That would work better than a no-entry sign, a bit of tape or a barricade. A fence could always be broken and cast aside. A scary superstition was much harder to shift.

Dillon had been summoned to the music room at morning break. The music teacher's sombre face lit up when he heard Dillon playing guitar and keyboards. "Do you read music?" he asked.

"Sort of."

Mr. Gregory smiled. "You mean, not very well."

Dillon nodded.

"So, how do you play?"

"I listen to a piece, then I play it."

"How many times do you have to listen before you take it in?" asked Mr. Gregory.

"Once."

"So, if I asked you to listen to a tune you haven't heard before, you could play it for me right away?"

Again Dillon nodded.

"That's impressive." Mr. Gregory thought about it for a moment and then said, "Why don't you come along at lunchtime? The school band's rehearsing and we can test you out – see if we can use your talent."

"All right."

But when Dillon saw the band, he knew he'd be snubbed, no matter how much he impressed them, no matter how much Mr. Gregory supported him.

The beefy student on drums was Cliff and he would persuade the others that they didn't need an extra member. As the rehearsal progressed, Dillon could see it in their manner. For a reason he didn't understand, the others regarded Cliff with a mixture of fear and sympathy. As soon as Dillon left the music room, Cliff would turn them against the newcomer.

After school, Dillon went to support Ainsley in the school's rugby match against a local side. Lining up at the edge of the pitch, there were a few other spectators, mainly parents. Not daring to join them, Dillon stood on his own. When the team ran onto the field, the supporter nearest to Dillon clapped and called, "Come on, Luke!" Dillon glanced at the man and noticed that the skin of his cheek was an ugly mixture of red and purple as if partly inflamed, partly bruised.

Before the game started, Dillon saw Luke, Simon and Cliff go into a huddle. He knew they were talking about him – even plotting against him –

because all three of them glanced at him twice. They also turned their hostile faces towards Ainsley, warming up with a run along the touchline. It wasn't just the biting cold that made Dillon shiver. Deep down, he felt that something was going to happen. He owed it to Ainsley to watch the game but decided that he'd leave before the end, before Luke, Simon and Cliff could put their plan into action.

But the three boys did not even wait for the final whistle. No one saw exactly what happened but, after one untidy maul, every player rose to his feet except one. With increasing horror, Dillon realized that the injured player was Ainsley. As the team's top kicker was carried off the pitch, Dillon was the only person in the crowd who knew that it wasn't someone in the opposing side who had put the boot in.

Dillon turned and walked away. As soon as he was out of sight, he ran.

7

In the cold wintry sunlight of Thursday morning, Dillon decided to cut through Bleakhill Top. He was going to do it to spite them all – the boys, teachers, his parents. He paused on the path that led to the cemetery and took a deep breath. An icy wind from deep in the dark heart of the wood chilled him. Yet he had made up his mind. He'd be jittery in the wood but comforted by being on his own. In Eastbridge, he preferred it that way. He stepped into the dark frozen wood that seemed to suck all life from the air.

Something made him stop again under the lime tree. It wasn't anything that he could hear, touch, see, taste or feel. It was something beyond his senses, as if the tree itself could beckon him. He turned and looked at it just as he'd seen the members of the school band viewing Cliff – with a mixture of fear and sympathy. The lime tree must have been diseased because its bark was split in places. The sores in its craggy trunk were protected by solidified sap, like wounds in skin caked with congealed blood.

Dillon spun round when he heard a growl. He wasn't fast enough to see what had made the noise, but he thought he heard an animal – perhaps a dog – loping off in the direction of the houses.

Leaving the path, he knelt by the sculpture on the

underside of the toppling tree. He could see now that the tree hadn't collapsed completely onto the ground because its upper branches had fallen into a young birch tree and caught there. He got the chisel out of his backpack and placed its cutting edge against the carved face. The width and shape of the blade matched the artist's strokes exactly, so Dillon was certain he possessed the carver's chisel. Making a hollow in the rotting leaves, near where he'd first found it, he laid the tool to rest, covered it over, and then continued the slog to school.

Miss Wright called him to her office and broke the news that it was even worse for Ainsley Scatterthwaite than Dillon feared. He was in hospital with a broken arm. The stud marks on his body showed that he had been thoroughly stamped on. "I just hope it was an accident and not done on purpose," she said. "I don't suppose you saw what happened, did you?"

"No."

"The team we were playing has got a reputation for violent behaviour."

Dillon kept quiet. He wasn't going to tell her that she should be looking for the culprits among her own side.

"Well, we're not expecting Ainsley back for a few days and I haven't managed to sort out another mentor yet."

Dillon detected faint signs of embarrassment in the Deputy Head as she fidgeted with a biro. Perhaps she had a hunch about what was going on after all. Perhaps she recognized that no one would want to be assigned to the new boy if they were going to end up in hospital.

"Miss?" Dillon dared to ask.

"What?"

"You said some council people got hurt in Bleakhill Top."

"Yes?"

"They went in to fix some vandalism, the local paper said. What vandalism?"

"I think you'll find it's another word for those offensive sculptures you talked about."

"Oh... I see. Why didn't they just say so?"

"No one mentions them. It brings bad luck, people believe. And, you have to admit, carving is a sort of defacement, so the trees *have* been vandalized."

"I suppose so," Dillon said.

He had mentioned the sculptures to Ainsley and now he lay in hospital. But Dillon doubted that an armful of bruises and a broken bone could be put down to mere bad luck. They had much more to do with the studs of malicious teammates.

It was only on his way home that Dillon realized Miss Wright's words didn't make sense. If the councillors had decided to chop down the spooky sculpture of the crushed man, it must have been shaped earlier. So how did the artist know that at some point in the future the inspector would be crushed? Maybe it was just coincidence. Or maybe the Deputy Head was mistaken. Perhaps some other damage had to be repaired and the sculptures were carved later...

Distracted, Dillon didn't see Luke and his pals hanging out at the newsagent until he was almost there. Feeling vulnerable without Ainsley, Dillon hurried up the footpath to Bleakhill Top. Behind him, Luke and Simon jeered and Cliff watched him in angry silence.

Bleakhill Top was becoming a private refuge for Dillon but he also had an idea that he wanted to check out. To satisfy his curiosity, he needed to take a closer look at the third carving before the afternoon became too gloomy.

As he walked along at speed, he realized that he was getting used to the muted atmosphere, the brooding menace and the tortuous path. He didn't feel at ease in Bleakhill Top but he was learning to avoid the worst of the holly, the grasping brambles and low branches. Having made a prompt escape from school, he arrived at the sculptures while there was still some light. Beyond the black silhouettes of the tall swaying branches there was a lingering blue glow. It was very cold, though, and Dillon's breath swirled like smoke.

Carefully leaving the path, Dillon clambered down the embankment towards the statue of the angry man and, beyond it, the figure that seemed to have wings. To keep his balance, he grasped branches, rocks, and even the muddy earth itself. Thankfully, once he'd reached the first sculpture, the ground became more level and he could walk without losing control.

At once, he realized that last time he'd been deceived by the dark. The third woodcarving wasn't an angel at all. Nothing like. It was sculpted in the same unmistakable cruel style. What Dillon had taken to be wings were actually flames. No wonder the man's face was a mask of torment. His back was burning, as if someone had set him on fire or…he'd been struck from behind by lightning. Dillon shuddered as he realized that he was looking at a wooden statue of James Aykroyd. But, according to Miss Wright, this figure had been fashioned before a bolt of lightning had felled the council worker.

Something here was uncanny, crazy or just plain wrong. Dillon didn't know which.

He could accept one coincidence. An artist might make one image that, by chance, came true. But Dillon couldn't believe that the same artist could do it twice. Surely the carver had made the sculptures *after* the woodland deaths. If they had been made before, the woodcarver was not just talented and mad, but also psychic.

Above Dillon, the sky had become deep purple. Before he lost all light, he looked around for a few minutes more. The emptiness was broken by the sound of his shoes snapping twigs and trees creaking, straining to break free of the soft soil. He headed for the spot where the noise of trickling water was at its loudest. If Ainsley was right, a murdered woman was weeping ghostly tears there. It could even be the place where she'd been beaten and buried. A few paces beyond the statue, Dillon was distracted by a massive fallen trunk of ash. At once, he knew that he was looking at the carver's final piece. It had to be the last one because it was unfinished. More than that, it was hardly started. Dillon couldn't make out what it was destined to be. Getting down close to the incomprehensible carving, he could make out a small human hand. It was held out, palm upwards, as if begging. Another part looked like the top of someone's head.

The hand was perfect except that there was still wood between the forefinger and thumb, making it look webbed. Feeling an irresistible urge to put it right, Dillon went back to the second sculpture near the path and retrieved the chisel. Returning to the incomplete piece, he knelt down and jabbed the sharp blade into the surplus wood. To scoop out a Vshape between the thumb and finger, he had to press down hard on the chisel. Of course, to do it properly, he would need a hammer to tap the chisel as he guided it through the timber. Even so, Dillon completed the hand but, in his final thrust, he slipped and made an accidental gash across the wooden palm. He cursed.

When he looked up, he was surprised. He'd been so absorbed in shaping the hand that he hadn't realized how dark it had become. Quickly, he pushed the chisel under the log and brushed leaves and twigs over it. Then he stood up and made his way out of the wood while he could still see where he was putting his feet. This time, he wasn't so scared. Perhaps he was getting used to the wood and the wood was getting used to him. Perhaps they were beginning to accept each other.

At home, the hot topic was tarmac. Some travelling workmen had called at the house during the day and offered to lay some new tarmac from the leftovers of a job they were going to do along one of the side roads. They'd agreed to come back on Monday evening.

Dillon's dad shook his head with a wry smile. "Is it one hundred per cent legitimate, this tarmac?"

Mrs. Carthy replied, "I'd be amazed if it was."

Dillon's mind was drifting back to Bleakhill Top when his dad asked him, "How're you getting on with your mate Ainsley?"

Dillon hesitated and decided that the truth was too complicated for his mum and dad. "Fine."

"Sure?" his mum asked with a frown.

Dillon nodded and then switched off again.

Outside, the wind stilled ominously and a dense fog settled on Eastbridge, deadening all sound and isolating the town. Inside, Dillon was gripped by the bewildering events in the creepy wood. Something was pulling him deeper into the mystery. He reckoned that the eyewitness interviewed by the local newspaper would know when the woodcarvings had appeared in Bleakhill Top. She might even know who had made them. He consulted the telephone book and a street map. Tomorrow he would visit Alice Burkinshaw.

8

A massive grey cloud, sagging under its heavy
burden of snow, hid the entire sky. Not used to
moorland weather, Dillon stared out of the
classroom window in amazement. He felt he should
be able to reach up and touch the cloud, as if
balancing a huge roll of cotton wool on his palm. He
nearly jumped out of his skin when Mr. Quillen bent

down and said directly into his ear, "Did you throw that chisel out?"

Truthfully, Dillon answered, "Yes." He failed to mention that he'd retrieved it afterwards.

The spidery teacher smiled. "You know, there's nothing wrong with the noble art of woodcarving. Just not with *that* chisel in *that* wood. We've got to channel you in the right direction. I can easily get some wood in. A lot of lime trees grow in these parts. They were planted to make charcoal for the steel industry but it's also good timber for carving. I've added it to my after-school art activities before. I can do it again."

Dillon shook his head, wondering how Mr. Quillen had jumped to the conclusion that he wanted to take up wood sculpture. "Thanks," he said, "but I'm not really into it."

Mr. Quillen did not reply. His expression suggested that he knew better.

The teachers seemed to be keeping a close eye on

Dillon. Several of them must have volunteered to substitute for the injured Ainsley. Mr. Gregory came to express his disappointment that there wasn't a place for him in the school band. "But you're welcome in the music room any time you like. I can even put you down for extra-curricular lessons if you like." The teacher's reddening cheeks told Dillon that the other members of the band had refused to play with him. In a corridor at break, Miss Wright checked that he didn't have the chisel with him and, at the same time, made sure he was in good spirits. The librarian asked him to be one of her assistants and his form teacher interviewed him during the afternoon break about his first week.

In the playground, the air was thick with snowballs. As soon as Luke, Simon and Cliff went near Dillon, the duty teacher whisked him away by asking him to run an errand. Before he left the noisy arena, he noticed that Simon's right hand was wrapped in a bandage. Maybe he'd sprained it in that same game of rugby. Dillon couldn't feel any sympathy for him.

After school, Dillon wondered whether he should visit Ainsley. He dismissed the idea right away. He didn't know either the hospital or Ainsley's house. It was a bad idea anyway. Ainsley had been punished for mixing with him so, if someone saw them together again, Ainsley might get into even more trouble. For Ainsley's sake, Dillon decided to steer clear of him.

Besides, Dillon had a different plan. He felt a strong impulse to return to the incomplete carving and, this time, to tackle it properly. Having already damaged its hand, he didn't want to make any more slips, so he needed the right tools.

He ignored his normal route, foiling any boys who might be waiting for him at the newsagent's shop. He went in the opposite direction, down onto the main valley road, where there was a small rundown shopping centre. In the hardware store, he selected the cheapest hammer he could find on the racks and took it to the counter.

The woman at the cash register eyed him suspiciously and then picked up the hammer. "What do you want this for, young man?"

"Chiselling," Dillon answered.

"Oh? Chiselling what?" she asked.

"Wood," Dillon replied. Feeling that he had to justify himself, and to put her off the scent, he added, "It's for an art project at school."

"Don't they provide what you need?"

"Most of the time, yes. But..." Dillon shrugged. "Not enough money."

Shaking her head, she put the hammer down as if she were about to refuse to serve him. Dillon guessed that she was dithering either because she believed that the young were always up to no good or because she mistrusted someone she didn't know.

Making up her mind to go ahead, she said, "You

don't want this. Not a metal head. You want a wooden mallet, medium size."

"Okay. I'll take one of them, please."

When Dillon walked out with his purchase in a plain brown paper bag, the shopkeeper's eyes followed him until he was on the street and out of sight.

The snow felt strange under his shoes. At first, it seemed about to take his weight but, as he leaned forward into a stride, the white stuff gave way with a satisfying crunch. He didn't attempt to go through Bleakhill Top because it was far too dark. Instead, he walked around it until he came to the terraced houses on the northern side – a slender barricade between town and wilderness. Counting the house numbers, Dillon walked along till he reached Alice Burkinshaw's home. He stood there for a few seconds and nearly raised a fist to knock on the front door but he didn't dare. He didn't dare to disturb her and, even if she had been in, he wasn't sure that he would be able to summon the courage to ask her his questions. Before some suspicious neighbour saw him loitering there and came out to ask what he was doing, he spun round and headed instead for his own house.

At the weekend, he didn't see much of his parents. They were out trawling the DIY shops, painting and decorating, and doing something very noisy with a drill, brackets and shelves. Dillon was left to his own devices. Telling his mum and dad that he was going to see Ainsley, he set out for the macabre wood with his new mallet in a plastic bag.

Despite the beautiful white coating of snow, Bleakhill Top was still unwelcoming. It seemed to be daring anyone to set foot inside. Dillon crept warily onto the unspoiled surface. The blackbird's dead body, with its bright orange beak and a light shroud of snow, was still on the path. In any other wood,

Dillon imagined that some animal would have taken it away as a tasty meal by now. The ground on his right reminded him of a ski slope but there wasn't a thick layer of snow. His boots went straight through it and into the soil underneath, leaving smudgy brown footprints as he edged his way down the steep part. Going straight to the unfinished sculpture, he scrabbled around under the snow and leaves until he found the chisel. Then he had all the equipment he needed – a mallet, a chisel and gloves to keep his fingers warm – but he doubted that he had the skill.

He didn't want his untrained hands to ruin what had already been formed from the ash, so he decided to try out his tools first on a branch. He looked around for a bough that was not too big, not too small, and at a convenient height. His gaze didn't linger for long on the lime tree. It had what he wanted and Mr. Quillen had told him that its wood was ideal for carving, but the tree unnerved him. Slicing into it was unthinkable, like cutting into his own flesh.

THE TORTURED WOOD

While he glanced around the branches, he spotted a black and white cat, almost perfectly camouflaged in this weather. The cat hadn't noticed Dillon because it was focusing all of its attention on a drab sparrow that was sitting on a higher branch. The cat was moving very slowly, deliberately and silently as it stalked its prey. At least Dillon understood now what had killed the blackbird. Nothing supernatural, just a cold-hearted cat. When it crouched down, ready to pounce, Dillon bashed his gloves together. At the sound of the dull thud, the bird flew away. There was no hint of an echo. The wood devoured the noise of his clap. The cat looked round and seemed to sneer at Dillon before it jumped sleekly to the ground. To show that it wasn't scared of him, it walked away unhurriedly, its delicate paw prints crossing the line of Dillon's isolated footsteps.

Near the unfinished carving there was another ash tree. It was still upright and from near the ground it split into two. Dillon decided that the smaller of the two trunks would be perfect for him but he wasn't sure how to begin. He imagined that real woodcarvers sketched an outline of their sculpture on the bark and chipped away, guided by their drawing. Dillon didn't know what he wanted to carve and he'd always been useless at sketching anyway.

Overwhelmed by the ridiculously difficult task, Dillon was in danger of giving up even before he'd started. Disheartened, he let out a weary breath and closed his eyes. There, in his mind, he saw a face, gazing closely at him. Shaken, he opened his eyes again and the snowy wood reappeared. He'd never experienced such a strong vision before and it shocked him. The hallucination seemed so real that Dillon expected to feel the face's warm breath on his skin. Inhaling deeply, he shut his eyes again. At once, the face returned. Dillon didn't think it was anyone he knew. It wasn't a particular person. It was just a plain face. Not happy, not sad, not angry, nothing. Lonely, perhaps, but that was all.

THE TORTURED WOOD

Dillon realized why the face had come to him. It was encouraging him – forcing him – to decide what to do. His first attempt at a sculpture would be an anonymous face. It felt right, not too ambitious for a first attempt. Even the best guitarist in the world had to start by forming a single chord. But Dillon still didn't know about the mechanics of woodcarving. In some ways, he wished that he could carve with his eyes shut tight. That way, the image that he wanted to create would be clear in his mind and some instinct might guide the chisel. It was a silly idea, of course. He had to see what he was doing. He decided to make a start by chipping away some wood, but to keep closing his eyes, so he could compare what he'd done with the virtual shape in his head.

The part of a face that stuck out most was the nose so that was where he began. The tip of the nose would be the outer layer of wood in the middle of the trunk. All he had to do was slice into the wood at the right angles around the tip to make a lifelike nose.

When he'd done that, he would arrive at the right depth for the face's cheeks, eyes and mouth.

He was surprised how easy it was to work with the chisel. He'd expected to struggle, pounding away at the handle with the mallet, but the steel blade slid smoothly into the timber as if it were penetrating wax. The tool was so sharp that it scooped out wood with just a few taps of the mallet. Its power was chilling. To Dillon, it seemed that the chisel knew what he wanted and was helping him.

He was soon happy with the shape of the nose and began to hollow out the gap beneath, making his way to the lips.

Dillon was concentrating so much that he didn't notice the passing of time. Occasionally, he'd stop, take a step back and examine his work. He'd close his eyes and compare it with his mental image. He was pleased with the sculpture that was evolving, delighted to discover that he had a knack for it. Ignoring for a while the creaking of trees and the sound of the hidden stream, Dillon was thrilled to see a human face taking shape. He took a step closer and shaved some wood from the right eyebrow, making it perfect.

He was so absorbed in woodcarving that he didn't realize that he was being watched.

9

A bark jolted Dillon back to reality. He spun round. Near the statue of the angry man, an Irish terrier was sitting, staring at him. It was totally still but it was a flesh-and-blood dog this time, not wooden. Amazingly, though, it looked exactly the same as the carved dog. It was sturdily built with a short and wiry brown coat. High on its forehead, its eyes were small, dark and deep-set, making it appear suspicious and bad-tempered.

A woman's cry punctured the silence. "Trooper! Here, boy."

The dog looked over its shoulder but refused to budge.

Dillon had never been frightened of dogs but he wondered if the terrier was waiting for reinforcements before it summoned the courage to attack.

Increasingly agitated, the voice shouted, "Trooper! Come out of there!"

A woman came along the track and climbed unsteadily down the bank. Grabbing hold of the terrier's collar, she muttered, "Nuisance! You know we don't come in here any more. It's not allowed." She was about thirty years old with a mark on her left cheek, maybe a mud stain or a bruise. She was clearly scared stiff to find herself in Bleakhill Top. The thought that someone else might be in the wood with her did not seem to have crossed her mind, so she didn't glance around and spot Dillon. Besides, she was focused on the dog and her own balance. It was only when Trooper growled – the same sound that Dillon had heard on Thursday morning – that she looked up. Startled at the sight of Dillon, she jerked back and gasped. "Oh!"

"Sorry," Dillon said. "I didn't mean to... you know."

Recovering from the shock, she said, "It's all right. Just that I didn't expect..." She glanced back at the path and then asked, "What are you doing?"

Dillon didn't know if he should admit it. "Er, nothing."

She looked at the tools in each of his gloved hands and then at the ash. "You're carving!"

Dillon nodded.

The woman looked even more agitated. "So that was the tapping," she muttered. Clutching Trooper's collar with one hand, she pointed at the face in the tree trunk with the other. "It's you."

Puzzled, Dillon turned back to his practice sculpture and studied it again. He could see what she meant. It wasn't his own face but there were similarities. The lips and eyes were certainly his. Dillon was staggered because the face in the ash was utterly blank, a model of solitude, like a broken prisoner gazing out from the tiny window of his cell. Dillon hadn't set out to portray himself and he didn't want anyone to think he was like that.

When he turned back to the woman, his mouth open, ready to deny it, she was leaving. Still clinging to the dog's collar, she let the sure-footed Irish terrier drag her up the slope. Up on the path, she hurried back towards the cemetery.

Still stunned that she had recognized him in the sculpture, Dillon shook his head, trying to convince himself that she was mistaken. To take his mind off the hurtful idea, he wandered over to the fallen ash where the gashed hand jutted out, pleading for help. For a few seconds, Dillon looked down at the budding sculpture, wondering if he was ready to take it on. Once more he closed his eyes and, just for a moment, he thought he glimpsed a part of what the original artist had intended. He saw a jumble of arms, legs and bodies that didn't make sense to him. The exposed hand was the tip of the carving. That flash of inspiration – or whatever it was – encouraged him to think that he could adopt the piece as his own and complete it.

But January days were short and cold. It was getting dark and he needed to warm up. The sculpture would have to wait till tomorrow. He put his mallet and chisel in the plastic bag and concealed it under the trunk. Then he retraced his steps to the track and followed the line of prints in the snow until he emerged from Bleakhill Top.

Dillon felt torn. He was afraid of the wood and yet he yearned for tomorrow when he could return and continue his carving. He wanted to tell his mum and dad all about it but he knew that, if he did, they'd ban any more visits. He knew he needed to make friends instead of spending most of his free time in a miserable wood. But he couldn't resist the pull of Bleakhill Top and modelling wood was easier than getting on with the other kids in this dreary place.

Over the holiday, Dillon had exchanged e-mails and virtual Christmas cards with his old friend, Matt, but that was nowhere near as good as the face-to-face chats they used to enjoy every day in Ipswich. Alone in the house, Dillon's best option was a phone call. "I wish we'd never moved," he complained to Matt.

"What's the problem? School? Home? Friends?"

"Friends? What are they?"

Matt said, "I see."

"In Eastbridge, the locals don't take kindly to strangers."

"Grim."

They talked and Dillon caught up with news

about the people and places he really liked. Then he asked, "How's the band?"

"Great," Matt answered brightly. "Gig tonight. We've got this girl on keyboards…"

"Girl?"

Toning down his enthusiasm, Matt said, "She's not as good as you, but she's okay."

Dillon could tell from Matt's voice that he was lying in an attempt to make him feel better. Maybe she wasn't as good musically but he guessed that Matt was keen for another reason. "Girlfriend, is she?"

"Pretty much, yeah."

Dillon forced himself to say, "Good for you." But he felt even more out of it. Life seemed to be passing him by while he was in another place, another time.

"Why don't you get yourself into a band up there?" asked Matt.

"Maybe," Dillon replied. He tried to sound optimistic but in reality he doubted that it would ever happen.

THE TORTURED WOOD

* * *

Sunday disappeared behind a wall of freezing fog. The snow underfoot had become crispy and Dillon suspected that he would not be able to do much carving before his fingers froze, even though he was wearing two pairs of gloves. He was squatting by the horizontal ash tree, tapping the handle of the chisel with his mallet. All around him loomed the threatening black silhouettes of the trees, poking out of a shifting grey haze. He felt like he was adrift on a ghost ship, listening to the water slapping against the sides and the ancient timbers creaking, with ragged masts overhead. He was sure about one thing: he had no idea where he was headed.

Despite being hindered by the thick padding on his hands, Dillon shaped a bent elbow faultlessly. It was easy with the awesome chisel. Dillon even questioned who was in charge. Was he controlling the chisel...or was it controlling him?

He glanced down at the tool and the scratched *DC*

caught his eye again. Could the chisel have been made for him all along? Much more likely, it had belonged to someone else with the same initials. He wondered if the previous owner also experienced mental pictures and had the same compulsion to carve.

In that frosty silence, he took no comfort in hearing a familiar sound – a growl and an unfriendly bark. At first, Dillon couldn't see the animal. It was unnerving, knowing that the hidden dog could leap out of the mist at any moment. Dillon stopped carving but he kept the tools in his hands – just in case. He stood upright and faced what he thought was the direction of the noise. But a dog was not the first thing he saw.

10

A human figure loomed out of the fog, a whirl of vapour dropping away from it as it glided towards him. For a second, Dillon's heart leaped as he thought he might be witnessing the murdered woman rising from her icy grave and closing in on him. Then he saw her extended arm, a dog's lead and the Irish terrier. Relaxing, he realized it was the woman who had taken Trooper away yesterday.

Keeping a tight grip on the lead, she said in a faltering voice, "At it again?"

Dillon nodded.

The woman looked past him, peering at the woodcarving, and then glancing around nervously. "I used to come here once."

"You're here now," Dillon pointed out awkwardly.

Trooper snarled at Dillon but the woman kept back so her dog could not reach him. "Not really," she said. "I only came to see if you were about."

"Oh? Why?"

She ignored his question. "I used to walk Trooper here. Quite a few people used to walk dogs in here and it were a short cut for the church and school. That were before…" Her voice faded away.

"Before what?"

She didn't answer immediately. She was silent for a moment and then said, "Before them trees started falling over. When it were safe." Her words came out in a flurry of steamy breath.

Right away Dillon spotted an opportunity. "A year ago?"

"Something like that."

He indicated the sculpture of the angry man standing indistinctly behind her. "Was that before the statues were carved?"

Her face glowed red and her free hand went to the bruise on her cheek. She answered, "No."

Dillon was baffled. "They were already here when the council workmen...you know...got hurt?"

"Yes."

"Really?"

She nodded. "I remember. I were going down to the shops to buy Christmas cards – not for this Christmas, the one before – and I heard a noise. Just like you yesterday. A sort of banging. Turned out it was him chipping away at a tree stump."

"Him?"

"A lad. A lot like you. He weren't from round these parts. A traveller." She turned unwillingly towards the carved oak as if she feared it. "He were carving my husband and Trooper, though I shouldn't think he'd ever seen them."

Dillon was amazed. "That's your husband? The one with the dog."

Avoiding looking at Dillon, she nodded.

"And it was a boy who carved him? And the other statues?"

She nodded again. "I liked to watch him. He'd cut a rough shape with a saw, then chisel it out. He didn't say much – never said his name – but he were good."

"Did he go to school here?" Dillon asked.

"The high school."

"Is he still around?"

The woman's face crinkled into a frown. "No." Changing the subject, she gazed again at Dillon's developing sculpture and said, "You're really like him. I wish I could watch you but..." Again, she looked around anxiously.

Dillon disliked the idea of someone peering over

his shoulder but he replied, "You can. I don't mind."
If she was going to help him understand what had
happened in the wood, he'd put up with a spectator.

"No. It's too dangerous."

Her behaviour surprised Dillon because she didn't
glance at the towering trees that had a habit of
keeling over. Instead, she looked fleetingly at the
sculpture of her husband. In the next moment, she
walked away and, led by Trooper, dissolved into the
churning clouds.

Dillon was mystified. Who was the young artist
and how could he have carved images of the future?
And where was he now? What had happened to him?
Dillon walked up to the man preserved in oak. He
could not bring himself to touch that fixed face, not
even with gloves. It was too stern and scary. He
could almost believe that the sculpture would open
its mouth, reveal a row of sharp teeth and clamp
them down on his tender fingers. Instead, Dillon
crouched down. The carved dog at the man's heel

was definitely Trooper. He was already baring his teeth, ready for a vicious attack. Dillon shivered and shook his head slowly. He had no reason to believe that the woman would be lying but he could not figure out why there was a statue of her husband in this lonely and forbidden spot.

Once again he concealed his tools by the ash and then headed for home and the comforting warmth of a gas fire.

On Monday morning, Ainsley was the centre of attention in the playground. Students were clustered around him, taking it in turns to write or draw on his plaster cast with felt-tip pens. Squinting in the harsh but cold sunlight, Dillon walked straight past. He wanted to join in, he wanted to see if Ainsley was all right, but he feared the reaction if he tried to mix. Instead, he headed for the library where he would be on desk duty for the Breakfast Reading Group.

THE TORTURED WOOD

It wasn't a tough job. Most of the pupils were messing around outside, skidding along the icy slide they'd made from one side of the playground to the other. Only a few had come into the library and they were more interested in warming themselves up and chatting about the weekend than taking books out. To pass the time, Dillon flicked through the only book on woodcarving that he could find in the Arts section.

Just before the bell announced the real beginning of school, Ainsley strolled into the library like some sort of celebrity. His broken arm was hooked across his body and encased in colourfully decorated plaster. "Hiya," he said to Dillon, not quite managing to sound cheerful.

"How is it?" Dillon asked, nodding towards his injury.

"All right."

Dillon felt like a misfit. "I don't suppose you want me to sign it."

Ainsley drew a deep breath. "Best not."

Dillon knew that Ainsley wouldn't want to carry around indelible proof that he was still friendly with the new boy.

Ainsley glanced around the library. "Still, looks like you're working it out without me."

"Yeah."

Ainsley lowered his voice and said, "Sorry. It's got a bit tricky for me. You know. Just watch out for Cliff Aykroyd. He's quiet but mixed up."

Dillon nodded. "Thanks. Don't worry about it."

Deciding that it would be wise to hang around at the end of the day until most of the gangs had dispersed, Dillon trudged along to Mr. Quillen's classroom where the after-school art activities were in full swing.

"Dillon Carthy," Mr. Quillen said, descending on him at once.

"I…er…just wanted to ask you something."

"What's that?" the art teacher replied with a sly smile.

"You said you'd done woodcarving before."

"Yes?"

"Who with?" Dillon dared to say.

The teacher's smile disappeared. "Oh, just a boy."

"What was he called?"

Mr. Quillen sucked in air and shook his head. "Can't remember. Why do you want to know?"

Dillon guessed that he knew the boy's name perfectly well. Warily, Dillon replied, "It doesn't matter. I just thought, if I ever did get into carving, maybe we could get together. You know, form a group or something."

Mr. Quillen nodded. "Commendable, but impossible, I'm afraid. He left the school some time back."

"Have you still got any of his work?"

"Let me see." Mr. Quillen paused as if he needed

time to think. Then he said, "Just a minute," and went to his cupboard. When he came back he was carrying his own head carved in a branch of lime. "This is the only thing I've got. His very first effort. Not bad for a practice piece."

Dillon nodded. The chisel's previous owner had probably fashioned Mr. Quillen's haunted bloodless face to convince himself that he was capable of carving, just like Dillon had tackled an anonymous face in Bleakhill Top. Dillon took the branch in both hands and examined it. He turned it over, looking to see if the artist had left his name anywhere, but there was nothing. "It's good," he said. "Did you show him how to do it?"

"Not really. I suggested a book, that's all. But he didn't need teaching. He had a natural gift."

"If this was just practice, what did he go on to do?"

Sidestepping the question, Mr. Quillen answered, "Nothing in school."

Dillon knew that he wouldn't be able to persuade the teacher to talk about the sculptures in Bleakhill Top. He seemed to think that it would be better if everyone forgot all about them. Not expecting to get anything else out of him, Dillon left. He was pleased. Had Mr. Quillen accidentally given him the information he needed to trace the young woodland artist?

11

Since moving, the Carthys had got into the habit of postponing their Sunday lunches until Monday evenings. His parents didn't prepare the roast at the weekend because they were too busy working on the house. This Monday, though, it was a disturbed meal. Every time they heard a heavy engine rumbling past, his dad or mum jumped up to check if it was the men with the dodgy tarmac.

They did turn up eventually. It was a team of two scruffy men and a boy. While the men spread one batch of the foul-smelling stuff across the drive, the boy brought them more from their truck. When he wasn't needed, he lounged on the doorstep, next to a large grimy wheelbarrow. The wind had turned during the day. The warmer southerly breeze had stripped Eastbridge of its white sheen but, now that the sun had gone down, it was again cold. Mr. Carthy stood in his overcoat, hands on hips, watching to make sure they did a thorough job. When Mrs. Carthy asked Dillon to take coffees out to his dad and the men, she got him to ask the boy what he wanted as well.

When the young man realized that Dillon was coming up to him, he flinched as if he was scared.

Knowing exactly how he felt, Dillon said, "It's all right. My mum's just wondering if you want anything to drink."

A year or so older than Dillon, the lad shook his head.

Dillon recognized the symptoms of distrust immediately. "I'm new here as well. I know what it's like."

The boy looked up at Dillon's face by lamplight, about to say something, when there was another shout. "More black stuff over here! Shift your backside, lad."

After he'd delivered three more barrow loads, the boy wandered back to the doorstep and plonked himself down. "Some of our families tried to settle here once." He shook his head miserably. "No chance."

Refusing to cave in to shyness, Dillon continued. "Did you go to Eastbridge High?"

He nodded. "Afraid so. Bunked off most of the time."

"I don't blame you," Dillon said quietly so his dad couldn't hear. "When was this?"

"Year before last."

"Where do you live now?"

"There's a travellers' park in Rotherham."

"When you were here, did you ever go into Bleakhill Top? The wood over there." Dillon waved an arm in the right direction.

"It's not illegal."

"It is now. Sort of. Anyway," Dillon said hesitantly, "did you see any woodcarvings?"

The boy watched his workmates pressing tarmac into place with a heavy roller. Making up his mind to answer the question, he replied, "More than that."

"What do you mean?"

"I mean, we did them. Well, not me, but..." Another yell from the workmen got him to his feet. He nodded towards the drive and said, "It's done."

"Please, just tell me who did the carving."

A look of utter sadness came to his face. "Darius."

Standing on the drive that was steaming slightly in the cold night air, one of the men shouted, "Come on! We're paying you to clear up, not natter like an old woman."

And that was it. Dillon went back inside with a tingling spine while outside his dad was counting ten-pound notes carefully into a workman's open palm. So, someone called Darius was the far-sighted artist! Dillon was no wiser about what had happened – and what was still happening – in the wood but, knowing a name, he felt much closer to the truth.

Whenever Dillon closed his eyes – in bed, in the bath, in Bleakhill Top, anywhere – the muddle of limbs and bodies that he aimed to create became clearer. Instinct now told him it was three people. The next morning, he had only a few minutes to shape a shoulder and a thigh because he was eager to get to the library in good time. Perhaps, if he could get away early from school, he could put in more work on the sculpture that afternoon.

The librarian had told him that the computer stored the names of the last three students to borrow each book. That way, if someone damaged a book, the school would have a good list of suspects. As library assistant, Dillon had easy access to the computer and he intended to make use of it. Hoping that Mr. Quillen had recommended the school's one and only book on woodcarving to Darius, Dillon swiped the volume past the reader and the computer let out a satisfied bleep. Right away, the monitor showed a list of three borrowers. The second was Darius Coe. He had returned the unpopular book at the end of the autumn term just over a year ago.

With the help of the young traveller he'd met last night, Mr. Quillen and the library's records, Dillon had at last put a name to the initials of *DC*.

The librarian walked past and, seeing the smile on Dillon's face, said, "You look a lot chirpier now. It's amazing what a good book can do."

He cleared the screen so she could not see what he'd been doing. "Yeah." But it wasn't a good book that was on his mind. It was Darius Coe. Dillon was fascinated by the boy who had come to Eastbridge High but had found it impossible to settle. Knowing what the locals were like, Dillon guessed that Darius had also suffered at their hands. Having first tried out his carving skills by forming Mr. Quillen's face, Darius had taken refuge in Bleakhill Top when it was still properly open. There, he had sculpted the trunks, somehow moulding the future, sometimes watched by that woman. The next bit – the important bit – was as shadowy as Bleakhill Top in cloud. Darius Coe had left no clue about his own fate.

Dillon thought there was a way of untangling the whole story. It was simple enough. All he had to do was to ask Darius. He was likely to be living in a travellers' park in Rotherham. Dillon just had to find him. That shouldn't be too difficult. For once, he would have to make an effort to speak to people.

The day went downhill as soon as he left the library. When Simon tripped him up in the corridor and sent him sprawling, some of the other kids laughed but many turned away. They were embarrassed by the treatment dished out to Dillon, yet unwilling to intervene.

When he opened his textbook in Spanish, he found a handwritten note inside. It read: *You stink, dog's breath*. Feeling knotted inside, Dillon stared at the cruel message. He hoped that it was the work of Simon, Cliff or Luke because he couldn't stand it if the other students thought like that as well. If they did, they were always going to keep their distance from him and he'd never make a friend. Unable to understand how anyone could be so hurtful, he screwed up the piece of paper into a tight ball.

By lunchtime, Dillon had had enough. He persuaded the nurse that he had a dreadful headache and that he needed to recover at home.

Of course, he didn't go home.

Angry and upset, he carved madly this time. Wood chippings flew in every direction as he moulded a boy's head. When he closed his eyes to see the image he wanted, Simon's nasty face filled his mind. Simon's expression was a mixture of shock and horror. Dillon didn't think too much about it. He simply chiselled quickly by intuition, letting the tool go about its task. He barely heard the groaning timber but could not ignore the sound of rushing water. It was louder than ever before and seemed to come from all around.

Putting the chisel and mallet down for a moment, Dillon walked round to the other side of the trunk. The earth was sodden with melted snow but there was no water in sight. He took another couple of steps away from the ash and suddenly the ground gave way under his foot.

12

Dillon caught his breath. Before he fell down into the sludge, he twisted and grabbed hold of a branch. Clinging desperately to the fallen tree, he tried to pull his foot out of the deep muddy hole, but the wet soil covering his shoe and ankle seemed to be sucking on his leg, refusing to give it up. He had a horrible feeling that a living corpse had a hand round his ankle and was dragging him down into the same grave. Panicking, Dillon got both hands on the branch and heaved with all his strength. Struggling against a vacuum, he slowly wrenched his foot out of the filthy mire, expecting to leave his shoe behind as a sacrifice to the greedy earth – or to the grasping dead. When he finally broke free, he was catapulted further into the network of dead branches.

Steadying himself, he stood there on one foot, breathing heavily with shock and effort. He was saturated with a sudden cold sweat. Sediment clung like tarmac to his leg from the shin downwards. But at least he could feel that his shoe was still in place. Scanning the ground in front of him, he could not see a trace of the spot where he'd been trapped. Slushy earth must have flowed back into the hollow and filled it up.

Shaken, Dillon hopped back to the horizontal trunk, sat down on it and examined his left leg. "Ugh!" He bent down for a stick and began the long job of scraping the brown gummy stuff away.

He felt miserable. Having spent so much time working on the bewildering sculpture over the last few days, he was beginning to feel at home in the wood. Yet Bleakhill Top had just reminded him that it wasn't to be trusted.

When he'd got rid of as much of the dirt as possible, he decided to go straight home. There, he would blame the state of his trousers on an accidental encounter with a puddle on the playing fields.

The next day, Mr. Quillen caught up with Dillon in the library and grasped him by the arm again. This time, he was even more agitated than before. "You weren't in school yesterday afternoon," he said.

"No," Dillon agreed. "I was feeling bad."

"Feeling bad, eh?"

"I saw the nurse."

Mr. Quillen still had hold of Dillon's wrist. "This is how it starts. I've seen it."

Dillon wasn't sure what the art teacher meant but

he guessed it was something to do with Darius Coe. He didn't want to admit that he knew about Darius, so he didn't reply.

"Are you absolutely sure you threw that chisel out?"

"Yes," Dillon answered. "I...er...wrapped it in newspaper and put it in the bin at home. Like you said."

Mr. Quillen released him but still looked into his face with suspicion bordering on disbelief.

The art teacher wasn't the only one who wanted to ambush Dillon on his way to the first lesson. Simon, Luke and Cliff appeared in the corridor as well but they backed off as soon as they saw Quillen. Calling after them, Mr. Quillen shouted, "Don't even think about it." Then he stared again over his glasses at Dillon. "You're as bad as them. None of you see where this is going. You just carry on. Blindly. I don't know where it's leading either, but I do know you've got to stop it right now."

Miss Wright walked past and enquired, "Everything under control, Mr. Quillen?"

"I think so," he replied. As soon as the Deputy Head was out of earshot, he muttered, "It's down to you, Dillon Carthy. Do you hear me?"

"Yes." He heard but he didn't understand. Yet Mr. Quillen's words had made up his mind. He would not carry on blindly in Bleakhill Top. He would follow the leads that might open his eyes to the events in the wood.

After another friendless day at school, he went back to Alice Burkinshaw's house at the edge of the treeless moor and this time he did raise a fist and knock on her front door. Fighting the urge to run away, he steeled himself as he heard a dog barking. A few seconds later, there was a noise somewhere inside and then a woman came to the door.

It was difficult to say who was more surprised.

Dillon stood there with his mouth open, unable to utter a word.

The woman with the Irish terrier exclaimed, "You!" With a look of fright, she glanced over her shoulder and then turned back towards her unexpected visitor. She whispered, "I can't talk to you," and slammed the door shut.

Dillon wandered away in a daze. The woman in the wood had been Alice Burkinshaw all along! She'd been a bit weird when she'd spoken to him in Bleakhill Top. At her own front door, refusing to say anything, she was even weirder. Dillon was disappointed but he had not run out of ideas. He had a different plan for tomorrow.

It was mid-January and the evenings were getting noticeably lighter. Dillon thought he had just enough time to fashion a little more of the sculpture, so he took a detour into the wood. This time he came to a halt by the statue of James Aykroyd.

A shiver engulfed his whole body as he remembered something that Ainsley had said. "Watch out for Cliff Aykroyd. He's quiet but mixed up."

James and Cliff Aykroyd! Then he recalled that newspaper article. *James Aykroyd...was born in Eastbridge and had always lived in the town. He leaves a wife and son.* Still staring at the awful howl that had been captured perfectly on James Aykroyd's face, Dillon nodded slowly. Cliff was mixed up because a year ago his dad had died violently in Bleakhill Top.

Another thought leaped into Dillon's brain. If Cliff Aykroyd had seen this sculpture, apparently celebrating his father's death, he'd be upset, probably angry.

Unable to concentrate on carving, Dillon went home, his head churning with unsettling ideas.

The mornings were still dark, the sun not yet ready to show itself any earlier. For Dillon, this morning would be different. Armed with a bus timetable, he skipped school and took a ride into Sheffield. A second bus took him swiftly into Rotherham. He was going to some derelict ground that, according to *The Sheffield Star*'s website, had become a travellers' campsite.

The collapse of heavy industry had left parts of Rotherham looking like a wasteland. There were huge buildings – once factories turning out goods – with all of their windows smashed, their roofs gone, walls covered with graffiti, and junk strewn everywhere. Surrounded by tall wire fencing, some of the disused factories were crumbling altogether. Great chunks of brickwork had crashed down to the ground. It was an ideal place for the council to locate travellers and their caravans because it was a space that no one else wanted.

As soon as Dillon walked uneasily onto the site, three burly men like bouncers barred his way.

"What do you want?" one of them said.

"I'm...er...visiting Darius Coe."

The three men looked at each other. "Darius?"

"Yes," Dillon replied, almost quaking as he stood there like a criminal before a harsh jury.

The men stepped to one side and one of them pointed further into the untidy community. "Fourth van on the right."

Dillon was so nervy that he forgot to thank the men. He had to force his legs to carry him in the right direction, and he kept looking one way and then the other as if he were crossing a road, expecting a sudden strike. Under his feet, dips in the concrete were filled with water and saturated litter. To one side, there was a small abandoned fridge and a ripped mattress. A little boy was chasing two small girls, making them scream playfully.

For some reason, Dillon was expecting a brightly painted caravan that could have been on show in a fairground, where the superstitious went to have their fortunes told. But it was nothing like that. It was a plain white caravan, not particularly smart but not rundown either. Taking a deep breath, Dillon was about to bang on the door when it opened wide.

13

From inside the trailer, a woman stared down at him, puzzled at first and then apparently pleased. Smiling, she stood to one side and said, "Come in."

Dillon was amazed. He didn't move. "Er... Is this where Darius lives?"

"Yes. Come in," she repeated. About the same age as Dillon's mum, she was wearing dazzling clothes and her short hair was jet black.

"Well…er…don't you want to know who I am and what I'm here for?"

The woman shook her head. "I don't know your name but I already know who you are and you're here to help my Darius. Come on. Don't just stand there."

Trying to control his nerves, Dillon climbed the step and entered the caravan. To his right, there was a small round table with five vivid candles and an ornate overhanging cloth. To his left was the cooking area and, beyond it, a couple of closed doors. The sound of an acoustic guitar came from behind one of them. On the floor, a gas fire hissed and blasted out a torrent of heat.

Directing him to a cushioned bench, the woman said, "If you haven't guessed, I'm his mum."

Dillon sat down and looked around, hoping that Darius would come in. But there was no sign of him.

Mrs. Coe nodded towards the source of the music. "All he does is play guitar to himself."

"Can I see him?"

"Of course, but there's something you have to know. You can see him but you won't hear."

"Pardon?"

She smiled, but it was an expression of sadness. "Since Eastbridge, he hasn't said a word."

"Really? But… What happened?"

Mrs. Coe shrugged. Standing, she said, "I'll bring him in." She went to the door and Dillon heard her say, "You've got a visitor. Come on." The music ceased but nothing happened until she went into the bedroom and took him by the arm, almost forcing him out into the open.

Darius's expression was completely blank. He didn't seem to be surprised to see Dillon. He wasn't curious, cross or concerned. Shorter than Dillon, he was about a year older and paler. He was gaunt, almost as if he were undernourished. He sat at the small round table and gazed right through Dillon.

At once, Dillon was reminded of the face he'd

carved in Bleakhill Top. His practice piece wasn't a self-portrait after all. It was Darius Coe, trapped in his prison of silence. Alice Burkinshaw had mistaken the image for Dillon because the two boys looked alike.

"You can talk to him if you like," Mrs. Coe said, "but…" Her voice trailed away.

Dillon, already ill at ease, felt tongue-tied. "Er… I'm Dillon," he stammered. "I go to Eastbridge High – just like you. I mean, like you used to. And I've seen your woodcarvings. I wanted to ask you about them."

It was hopeless, like talking to a doll. Darius was staring back at him, possibly seeing something beyond him. There was no indication that he was listening and no attempt to respond.

With a hopeless look on his face, Dillon turned to Mrs. Coe.

She shrugged. "You can ask me."

"Do you know about Bleakhill Top?"

"My Darius told me everything up until that last time – till he said no more," she answered.

Trying to forget his unease, Dillon said, "I think Darius carved an angry man and his dog. They were probably the first ones he did in the wood. Do you know why he did them?"

"Let's have a drink. Tea?"

"No, thank you. I don't really like it." Dillon felt awkward. He knew Mrs. Coe was trying to be friendly and he didn't want to appear rude.

Filling the kettle and placing it on the gas stove, she said, "You'll like mine." Leaning against a cupboard that stretched from floor to ceiling, she added, "Yes, I know why he carved them. He's still got the scars on his legs."

"Sorry?"

"He went to your school all right. Well, sometimes he did. He skived off a lot. He wasn't happy there and he preferred to go to the wood and carve. All the dog walkers – and Christian folk going to church – ignored him or told him off for vandalizing the woods. They even called him things. Dirty gypsy, and worse. Darius hated it. But there was one woman who'd watch him carve. She was impressed, I guess, and she chatted nicely to him. The only one, mind."

It seemed strange to Dillon to be talking about a boy who was sitting there in the same room, taking no obvious notice. "Was it Alice Burkinshaw?"

"I don't know names," Mrs. Coe replied. "Darius said, when he'd finished, she was amazed that he'd made a likeness of her husband and his dog. Right on cue, that's when he turned up, this husband. Apparently, he was furious to see his wife with Darius when she was supposed to be home from church. Got into a temper, he did, and set his dog on my Darius. Dreadful man. After, I heard some whispers saying he'd killed his wife but that was silly. People will talk. Darius saw him hit her, though. Darius never saw her again after that."

So, the murder was just gossip. When Dillon had seen Alice Burkinshaw appear like a phantom from the mist, she was as real and alive as anyone else – but bruised by a brutal husband. At least he understood her nervousness now.

Dillon glanced at the silent Darius and then looked back at his mother as she poured boiling water into an old-fashioned teapot. The caravan – already smelling sweet – filled with the strong scent of herbs. "I can hardly believe it, but Darius was carving the future then?"

Leaving the tea to brew, Mrs. Coe replied, "Maybe that seems strange to you."

Dillon nodded.

"It shouldn't. Oh, the future keeps some secrets. Just as well, isn't it? Life would be dull without surprises. But my Darius always had a pretty good feel for it. I guess he gets that from me." She fingered a crystal pendant that rested on her chest.

Her remark brought an unwelcome notion into

Dillon's mind. When he closed his eyes to visualize a carving, was it the future he was seeing – like Darius before him? After all, he already shared initials, and a talent for music and wood sculpture with Darius. And, of course, rejection. Perhaps he shared foresight as well. Trying to shake off the idea, he said, "I think he carved a council inspector next."

Mrs. Coe handed Dillon a thin china cup filled with a spicy brew. "Get that down you. You look like you need it."

"Thanks."

"I know a name this time because it got in the paper. Hinchliffe. Crushed by a tree, he was. Exactly as Darius pictured it."

"And James Aykroyd?"

She nodded. "A quick way to go, lightning, but not pretty. Eastbridgers didn't like the statues. Offended by them, I heard. So, they stopped people going in the wood and tried to get rid of them. Like erasing pencil marks." Mrs. Coe shook her head sadly. "You can't rewrite a future foretold."

To calm himself, Dillon sipped the hot drink and, much to his surprise, its flavours burst pleasurably in his mouth. "Mmm."

"I told you," she said. "Another prediction come true."

"But what happened to make Darius…like he is?" asked Dillon.

Mrs. Coe hesitated, as if wondering how best to answer. Then she replied, "There's only one thing I know. Whatever they did to him, they'll do to you too."

Dillon almost slopped his herbal tea.

"Sorry, but I had to warn you." Gazing directly into his face, she continued, "I have to tell you something else. You can stop it. You can help Darius, help Eastbridge. It depends on what you do."

"How do you mean?" Dillon asked.

She shrugged. "I don't know. But that's what I feel in my bones."

Dillon tore his eyes away from Mrs. Coe and gazed instead at Darius, pleading for a response, for some sort of support.

Under the surface, something seemed to stir in Darius. He put a hand to his face and let out a faint groan. Very quietly, he uttered, "Watch for the slide."

14

On the way back to Eastbridge, Dillon had plenty to chew over but Darius Coe's comment about a slide left him completely confused. There was a slide in the kids' playground but Dillon didn't know if that had anything to do with it. Or was Darius thinking about an icy surface, like the one at school on Monday morning? Or had a year of silence affected his brain? The whole encounter with the Coe family was so weird that Dillon wanted to laugh it off as ridiculous. But everything that Mrs. Coe had told him fitted with the facts. However much he wanted to, he could not dismiss the Coes as cranks.

Now, one question occupied Dillon's mind more than any other. What had happened to affect Darius so drastically? Dillon was desperate to find out because, if Mrs. Coe was right and it was also going to happen to him, he needed to work out what to do. But, no matter which way his mind went, he couldn't figure it out. He had just one clue: the unfinished carving in the ash tree. If it was like Darius's other pieces, the tangled sculpture was the key because it would reveal the future.

As the bus bumped along a pot-holed road, Dillon closed his eyes. At once, he saw Simon. It seemed to Dillon that Simon was below him, thrashing about, as if madly trying to clamber out of a bath. There were two outstretched arms as well. Only one belonged to Simon. Dillon couldn't see the other person. It was like looking at a blurred photograph with one of the figures cut off at the shoulder, leaving a disembodied arm.

Dillon knew with total certainty that he needed to work on the sculpture as quickly as possible.

When he got back to Eastbridge, he squeezed in an hour of carving in Bleakhill Top. The chisel had always seemed comfortable in his hand yet Dillon was still wary of its uncanny power. He remembered thinking, before he knew anything about Darius, that its previous owner must have been mad and cruel. Dillon didn't want to end up like that. And he certainly didn't want to end up unable to utter a word. He glanced at his watch and then went to the end of the road that led to Ainsley's house. There, he waited. Knowing now that Cliff was James Aykroyd's son, Dillon wanted to check out something else with Ainsley.

When Ainsley caught sight of him, he looked

carefully over both shoulders to make sure no one was watching. When he was satisfied that nobody would see him talking to the enemy, he dragged Dillon behind a hedge with his good hand. "What is it?"

"Sorry," Dillon muttered. "I just need to know Luke's name."

Ainsley looked puzzled.

"His surname," Dillon explained.

"Oh. Oxley. Luke Oxley."

Immediately he recognized it. Two of the council workmen who were burned alongside James Aykroyd were called Oxley. The three chief bullies must be the troubled sons of the council workers who were hurt or killed in Bleakhill Top. Remembering that Mrs. Coe had said that the council inspector was called Hinchliffe, Dillon decided to show off. "And I bet Simon is Hinchliffe."

"No," Ainsley replied. "Why?"

"I've figured it out. At least I thought I had," said

Dillon in a low urgent voice. "You said Cliff had had it rough. That's because his dad died in the wood. Luke's dad got burned but survived. I think I saw him – with a disfigured face – at the rugby match when you broke your arm. Anyway, Cliff and Luke had a go at Darius Coe – did something to him – because he was an outsider and he made cruel pictures of the accidents. They got him before he finished another carving."

It was a few seconds before Ainsley could answer. "No wonder you weren't in school. You've been digging around."

"It's true, isn't it?"

"We don't talk about it," said Ainsley stubbornly.

Keyed up, Dillon said, "Oh, come on."

"Why?"

"Because I'm next. You know it. They're gunning for me."

Ainsley sighed, made sure again that no one was spying on them, and then said quietly, "Everyone thought the things in the wood were right ugly, that's all. That's why they wanted to be shot of them. But when Cliff's dad were struck by lightning, Cliff were first to work it out. Darius Coe were making fun of them that was killed, insulting Eastbridgers. Cliff got together with Luke – because his dad and uncle got hurt at the same time – and they teamed up with Simon…"

"Why Simon?"

"A tree fell on his sister's bloke…"

"And he was Hinchliffe, the council inspector."

"Yes. Cliff, Luke and Simon decided they'd do something about it together. They went off to catch Coe red-handed in Bleakhill Top."

"What did they do?"

"I don't know."

"You really don't know?" Dillon checked.

"No."

Dillon believed him. "Pity."

"You shouldn't know all this," Ainsley said. "It's

not good for you." He looked into Dillon's face and asked, "Have you been going in the wood?"

Dillon nodded.

Ainsley breathed in deeply. "Just don't do any carving."

"Too late," Dillon blurted out. "I can't stop now."

Ainsley shook his head in despair. "You'd better start saying your prayers, then."

After dinner, Dillon pleased his parents by announcing that he was going to see Ainsley again. He wasn't really, of course. He felt sorry that he was getting into the habit of telling lies. That was another thing that Eastbridge was doing to him. It was making him dishonest. But he just couldn't tell them the truth.

"Fine. Good for you," his mum said.

Predictably, his dad asked, "Have you done your homework?"

THE TORTURED WOOD

"Yes." Dillon paused and then added, "It's down a dark lane, so I'm going to take a torch. All right?"

"Help yourself from the garage."

Dillon took his dad's most powerful torch and then set out for Bleakhill Top. It was a cold and clear night. The full moon was bright, as big as a football. It was foolish, Dillon knew, to attempt to carve late at night by torchlight but he felt compelled to complete Darius Coe's image as quickly as he could because it would show him what was going to happen.

The torch formed a corridor of light in Bleakhill Top and Dillon picked his way carefully along it, past the skeleton of the lime tree. A crow took off from one of its dead branches, flew across the moon and disappeared into the night.

Dillon worked inside a glowing bubble. It was difficult and odd because the shadows of one part of the sculpture fell on another, making it hard to fathom, but the uncanny effect didn't blunt his imagination. It probably helped.

Dillon was disturbed only by night-time sounds. Clicking, creaking, the occasional hoot, and the ever-present trickling noise. Dillon kept looking around but he could see nothing beyond his bubble. The glow of the torch seemed to push the wood away but twice a creature – almost certainly a bat – flew swiftly through his sphere of light. It was scary to think that anything could be out there, maybe some wild animal from the moor. It could be lurking at the edge of darkness and he would never know until it pounced on him. He just hoped that Bleakhill Top would tolerate his presence.

He concentrated on shaping the eyes of another face knowing that, in the shadows, he would not be able to make out who it was. By daylight, though, he hoped he'd be able to stand back, view his evening's work and unravel the future.

In a candlelit caravan in Rotherham, a boy opened his eyes in the middle of the night. "Mum? You know that boy who came here?"

At once, Mrs. Coe was out of bed and, eyes filling with water, rushing to her son's side. "Darius, honey. I knew you'd speak again. I just knew! There'd be a visit from a boy like you and then you'd speak. That's what I've always believed."

Darius ignored her comment, as if talking were totally unremarkable. "Will he be all right?"

"I can't say, honey," she answered. She clasped her hands and wiped away the tears of joy because her son had returned to her after a year's absence.

"Why can't you?"

"It depends what he does. What will those boys do to him, Darius? What did they do to you?"

Darius didn't respond.

"You turned up after three days, dehydrated and half-starved. We all saw the bruises. Your arms were chewed up something dreadful. They beat you up. But you were no stranger to fights. There was more, wasn't there?"

Still Darius refused to answer.

Mrs. Coe put her hand lovingly on his cheek. "It's okay. That's enough for now. The words'll come when the scars heal."

15

Miss Wright was getting really animated, to show how seriously she regarded Dillon's second offence. "Last week I said it wasn't easy to fit in midway through the year. Especially in a tight-knit community like this one. I appreciate that. But bunking off won't help. Running away from your problems won't make them go away. It could make matters worse." She paused to take a breath. "I blame myself. I should've persisted with a new mentor. I blame your fellow students, but I can't make them accept you. And I blame you. Perhaps you think I'm being harsh but it's the truth. You've got to make a stab at integrating. Okay, the thing with the school band didn't work out and Ainsley's accident didn't help. Becoming a library assistant was a good idea but I think you're just using it to hide away. You didn't take up the offer of after-school art or music practice. If you had, you'd have met like-minded students."

Dillon stood in her office, head bowed, and took it all. At least, while she was lecturing him, he was out of harm's way.

"Do you like being a loner?" she asked provocatively.

Dillon shook his head.

"No, not many do. So, what are you going to do about it?"

THE TORTURED WOOD

He didn't want to use up valuable carving time but he hoped to finish the woodland sculpture this weekend so he muttered, "I'll go to music after school next week." That seemed the easiest way to pacify the Deputy Head. He even tried to convince himself that it had a chance of working.

"All right, Dillon. I'm going to put you on a yellow card. Think yourself lucky it's not red. But it turns red if I don't see you in the music club. Got that?"

"Yes, Miss."

"It's for your own good. I'm sure you can settle in, Dillon, and I've seen enough to think you can be a real asset to the school. And, once you're bedded in, I think the school can give you plenty of opportunities to stretch yourself – and enjoy your time here. Let's aim for that, eh?"

Dillon nodded without conviction.

A malicious black cloud rolled over Eastbridge, spitting hailstones and lightning. The atmosphere was suddenly alive with thunder, long and loud. The storm had taken hold of the air and given it a thorough shaking, intent on using it as a brutal battering ram to scatter the pupils of the high school. The whole place quaked. The students in the yard made a mad dash for the side door into the school while the thunderstorm threw its stones violently into the puddles of the playground.

Every second at school seemed like a storm to Dillon. The thunder made his insides quiver. When he merged with the tide flowing towards the building, he didn't get very far before someone barged into him and bowled him over. It was Simon, but this time it seemed to be an accident. Dillon splashed down in a pool, bombarded with hail.

Simon said, "Oops! Sorry," and put out his scarred hand but, when he saw who he'd felled, he withdrew his offer of help and joined the rush to get indoors.

The last to leave the playground, Dillon got to his

feet on his own and jogged towards the side door but Simon had slammed it shut, keeping him out.

Not even Dillon's personal squad of minders on the staff could save him from this latest humiliation. As the hail turned to pelting rain, he felt like giving up and going home because everyone and everything seemed set against him, but the Deputy Head's warning rang in his ears. He walked round the outside of the school to the main entrance. There, the receptionists would make sure he could get in. Bedraggled, physically and mentally bruised, soaked, his hair flattened against his head and water dripping down his neck, he tramped back into the hateful place.

The lashing rain had ceased by Saturday morning but the road from Dillon's house to Bleakhill Top was a mass of dirty puddles. On the moor, the stream that headed into Eastbridge had been transformed from a trickle into a torrent. Dillon looked at it for a while, wondering where all that water went, before he strode into the cemetery.

The wood was particularly slippery and unsafe. To the sound of loud gurgling water, Dillon worked on the ash tree. Whenever he shifted his position, he was very careful where he put his feet to make sure he got a good grip. He didn't fancy having a leg sucked into another muddy pothole.

The second figure of the sculpture was now absolutely clear in his mind. It was Luke. Dillon had only to chip away a little more timber here and there to give the wooden face the torment that Luke deserved. Then Dillon began to give an identity to the third person in the piece. He did not doubt for a moment that it was Cliff. The arms and upper body were already in place. The rest merged with uncut wood and that felt right. Dillon knew that the sculpture would be complete when he finished Cliff's face. It would be a startled expression, staring up at the sky like a drowning man taking his last breath before going under.

As he knelt down, that first hand, formed by Darius Coe, caught Dillon's eye and he hesitated. Last week, in his amateurish attempt to cut out the wood between forefinger and thumb, Dillon had slipped and cut into the palm. The gash was still clear and Dillon stared at it in horror. It was exactly the same wound that he'd seen in the playground yesterday on Simon's hand.

For a few seconds, the full meaning of the parallel didn't strike him. When it did, it was like a sickening blow to the stomach. Going as white as a sheet, he dropped the mallet and his hand shot to his mouth. "No!" His cry was swallowed by the wood around him.

It could be a coincidence that Dillon had sliced into the palm and, shortly after, Simon had turned up with a cut hand. But Dillon barely gave it a thought. He was convinced that there was more to it than chance. At that moment, he was certain that the sculptures were not just an interpretation of the future. They were the trigger that brought it about.

He believed that Darius had carved the cruel images to get his own back on the local residents. Darius hadn't really predicted that a tree trunk would crush Mr Hinchliffe or that lightning would kill James Aykroyd. He was making it happen. He was shaping not just the statues but also the future. Now, Dillon was also certain that he could do the same. He could take the chisel and merely run it across Luke Oxley's wooden cheek to slash the boy's face. It also dawned on him that the police wouldn't be able to touch him. He could repay those who had wronged him and get away with it. He didn't even have to go near them to gain his revenge.

He had such control over them! He had power over their lives – and deaths. It was enticing and scary at the same time. In seconds, if the mood took him, he could slice off a hand, disfigure a face, or even slit a neck. He could take out his frustrations on the three bullies with no risk to himself. It was so tempting. After all, they deserved it, didn't they? And after that, he could carve more Eastbridgers – anyone who was mean to him – and do whatever he wanted to them.

Bending down again and picking up his mallet, he remembered what Mrs. Coe had said. "You can stop it. You can help Darius, help Eastbridge. It depends on what you do." He wasn't sure exactly what she had meant but he suspected that she'd been talking about his newly discovered power. But he was certain about one thing: he could not stop carving the chaotic scene in the ash. Working with the chisel had become a habit, like lying. He had to complete the sculpture. He had to make the future.

Chisel in one hand and mallet in the other, he squatted down to work on Cliff's face. When Dillon closed his eyes, he saw agony etched there. But, Dillon realized, Cliff Aykroyd had already been through torture because of the accident that Darius had fashioned for his dad. Perhaps it was the lightning strike that had made Cliff into the spiteful boy he was now. So why should Dillon heap more torment on him?

Yes, it would be easy to destroy Cliff but Dillon didn't really want that. He wasn't as nasty as the boys who taunted him. Eastbridge might be making him dishonest but it hadn't yet made him cruel. Taking his revenge through the woodcarving would be much easier for him than to offer sympathy and understanding, but in his heart he knew that was what he should do. He should put things right rather than solve his problems by eliminating anyone who crossed him.

As he put the chisel against the timber, Dillon wondered if he had to obey the pitiless image in his head. Why should he? Surely the sculpture did not have to be like that. He should be able to make it to his own design. He slanted the chisel differently, unnaturally, to form a different expression on Cliff's lips. He tried for a faint smile of relief. Yet, for the first time, he didn't feel at one with the chisel. The tool was resisting Dillon's idea.

Alarmingly, behind him, there was the deafening noise of tearing wood. A thick bough of a chestnut slowly peeled away from the trunk and crashed to the muddy earth. Then the soil itself began to move and it seemed as if the whole tree was attempting to wrench itself from the ground. Dillon wanted to jump up and run to safety but he thought that he might slip on the muddy surface and fall flat on his face. He might even stumble into the tree's path and be crushed. So he stayed where he was, crouched down low, raising his arms to protect his head in case any branches came down on him.

Luckily, when the chestnut tilted, it leaned away from Dillon. He could feel the ground rippling underneath him as the roots seemed to yank, tug and twist. It felt like an earthquake. Then, with a colossal crash, the tree came down on its neighbours, smashing through their branches. The trunk crunched against the statue of James Aykroyd and pushed it to a crazy angle. A huge mound of soil rose up into the air, clinging to the chestnut's exposed roots.

For a minute, Dillon calmed himself, taking control of his breathing again. Trying not to be put off, he turned his attention back to his sculpture, still determined not to yield to the chisel. He was fed up with all these grief-stricken expressions. He tilted the chisel awkwardly in the hope of making one corner of the lips turn up wistfully. The art of carving didn't seem so easy when the chisel wasn't willing him on. Still defiant, Dillon hit the handle with his mallet and at once something utterly dreadful happened. In his hand, the chisel shattered.

16

Darius Coe let out a cry and sat up sharply.

"What is it, honey?" his mother asked, rushing to his side.

"I don't know, but..." He shook his head. "I think he's trying to change things."

"Dillon, he said his name was," Mrs. Coe replied. She hesitated, a worried smile on her lips, before adding, "Good for him. He's a brave lad."

Darius nodded.

To make sure her son didn't slip back into silence, she asked, "What's he trying to change, Darius?"

"The ones who'll come for him."

Mrs. Coe nodded. "Some other boys?"

"Yes."

"The same ones who got you?"

"I think so," Darius answered.

"What'll they do to him?"

"They'll kick him around, strip him and tie his arms round a tree trunk with a rope. They'll leave him there – strapped to it – as a joke."

Mrs Coe looked at Darius in sympathy. "So that's what happened to you. I should've seen it but I didn't."

"He'll be cold and hungry, alone in the wood."

"You were trapped there for three days. The nights must have been awful."

"He'll be frightened and humiliated."

"His mum'll be frantic as well." She touched her

son's cheek again, wiping away a single tear with her thumb. "You'd gone off for days before and come back, no harm done, but I knew something was wrong. I just didn't think of looking in the wood. How did you escape, honey? Did someone find you and let you go?"

Darius lowered his head. "He'll have to rub the rope on the bark till it wears through."

Mrs. Coe sighed. Now, after all this time, she understood what had happened to Darius. "So," she said, "that's how your arms got in such a state."

Darius turned and hugged his mother fiercely.

Dillon was staring in shock and horror at what he had done. It was only a chisel, he knew, but it was probably unique. He felt like he'd been parted from a best friend. The wooden handle lay in countless pieces, scattered over the tangled sculpture and the earth. The blade had launched itself into the air and dropped onto loose soil near where he'd lost his footing on Tuesday. It had sunk without trace right away.

He dithered for a few moments, wondering what to do. But the urge to complete the sculpture was as strong as ever. And Cliff's face was a mess, like a smudged painting on wet paper. Making up his mind, Dillon set out for the hardware store. He didn't know if he could carve with a different chisel, but he was determined to try.

Spewing rainwater from their tyres, cars surged along the shabby main road on their way to Sheffield's huge shopping centre. On the pavement, some boys were hanging out, making a nuisance of themselves. With alarm, Dillon noticed that Cliff, Simon and Luke were among them. Quickly, he darted into the shop and hoped that he hadn't been spotted.

Once he'd bought a new chisel with a blade similar to his old one, he slipped out again, past the newsagent's and sneaked back up the track into

Bleakhill Top. He glanced behind him anxiously a few times, but no one seemed to be following him.

When he clambered past the trees, they groaned as if tired or fed up with his frequent comings and goings. It seemed that Bleakhill Top had had its fill of human visitors.

By the horizontal ash, Dillon surveyed his work. In the last few days, he had converted Darius Coe's puzzling beginnings into a nightmare jumble of three bodies. With a sense of foreboding, Dillon kneeled down with the new chisel and attempted to reshape the final part – Cliff's formless face – into something that wasn't in his head when he shut his eyes. It was too late to alter the horrified expressions on the other two faces but on the third Dillon wanted to show not just fright but hope as well.

It was really difficult to work against his instinct. Shape had flowed effortlessly from Darius Coe's chisel but, with this new one, Dillon struggled to make any recognizable features. Even so, he persevered.

At first, he didn't even realize that he wasn't alone. It was only when he looked up, frustrated with the chore, that he saw Cliff, Simon and Luke in a line, watching him with contempt on their faces. He gasped. They must have seen him near the shop and followed him into the wood after all. He also saw something beyond their hate. In their eyes, he could see that they were afraid. Dillon didn't know if they were scared of him – the outsider – or scared of being in Bleakhill Top.

Chillingly, Cliff muttered, "You're mocking my dad as well." His head turned slightly towards the statue of the man in flames, now slanting absurdly, but he didn't dare to look at it.

"No," Dillon said, "It's not like that. I..." He stopped trying to defend himself when he spotted the rope dangling ominously from Luke's hand. Besides, he thought it might be a bad idea to encourage them to take a closer look at what he'd been doing. If they recognized themselves, he dreaded to think what they'd do.

An ugly smile on his lips, Luke held up the blue nylon rope and said, "Yes. You don't like the look of this, do you? Tough. It's what you deserve for fooling around in here."

"You told me to come this way in the first place."

"Only to scare you," Luke retorted. "Not to start this again."

"What did you do to Darius Coe?" Dillon asked, his voice barely more than a stutter.

Simon laughed. "Stupid gypsy."

Luke said, "See that tree over there?"

Dillon did not really have to look. He knew. It had to be something to do with that warped and bleeding lime tree.

Jiggling his hands, Luke made the nylon rope dance. "He spent a good few days attached to it. Just like you're going to do. And we're going to take your clothes, so you get the full benefit of the cold."

When the three of them rushed at him, Dillon grasped the chisel defensively, holding it out threateningly in front of him.

Simon didn't hesitate. He slammed into Dillon and knocked him over. He yanked the tool from Dillon's hand and threw it away. "Coe was soft as well. Like you, too soft to use it." In a squatting position, his shin was jammed against Dillon's ribs and he had both fists on Dillon's coat, pulling it tight around his neck, throttling him.

Without a weapon and short of breath, Dillon tried to jerk out of Simon's grasp, swinging his arms and kicking out with his legs. His hands clenched into fists and he hit out wildly. His foot crashed into something solid – his own carving. When his leg recoiled from the blow, his knee struck Simon on the back of the neck.

Simon let out a yowl, clutched his neck and leaped away from Dillon.

All three boys were so angry, their faces glowed red.

Luke said, "I'm not scared of you." He threw the rope over a convenient branch then he flew at Dillon and punched him viciously in the stomach.

Gasping for air, Dillon dropped to his knees. The back of his head and coat, his elbows, knees and hands were plastered with brown sludge.

Up above them, near the path, one of the younger birches lost its grip on the loose earth. It bowed down and then toppled over. Without the birch to support it, the dead tree with the sculpture of the crushed man completed its fall at last. It seemed that time had been unfrozen and the image of the council inspector finally disappeared, buried in wet soil.

Even the angry man carved in oak shifted his position, leaning and twisting to one side.

Still focused on Dillon, Luke cried, "Let's get him!"

17

Just as the three boys rushed towards him, there was a heart-stopping rumble that seemed to well up from the earth itself. The sound got louder and louder as it came to the surface. With a fearful scraping and churning noise, the ground next to Dillon and the three boys tore apart. The restless land opened to reveal what had been a swollen underground stream.

Suddenly, the rift was a river of mud and water cascading down the hillside.

At once, the lime tree collapsed into the landslide. The ruthless silt tossed the trunk over, pulled it under and then carried it towards the bottom of the valley as if it were a mere toy.

Dillon fell to his knees, stranded on a piece of stable ground. Trembling, he dared to crawl forward and take a peek over the lip. It was like looking down into some sort of hell. Below him, there was a torrent of filth. Awesome swirls sucked at the earth, widening and deepening the channel, tumbling over each other in their frenzied downhill race.

The flood had also tried to claim the other boys. The collapsing earth had tipped them over the edge of the trench in a jumble of arms, legs and bodies. Luke and Cliff were hanging by their fingertips on to the bank of the mudslide, but Simon hadn't been so lucky. Taken by surprise, he hadn't managed to get a grip on anything solid. A greasy tree root that was slowly slipping out of his left hand was the only thing preventing the brown slime from whisking him away and drowning him. Already, mud had devoured his legs. The moving mire came up to his waist and threatened to engulf his chest. Panicking, he screamed. His outstretched right hand became that pleading scarred palm of the last woodcarving.

Dillon grabbed the ash with his left hand and, praying that the ground under him would not budge, leaned out over the edge in an attempt to clutch Simon's wrist in his right fist. Yet, when Simon's petrified eyes saw that it was Dillon who was trying to snatch him to safety, he hesitated. In that instant, it seemed that Simon was going to withdraw his arm, just as he had done in the playground yesterday, and take his chance with the landslip. By the time he realized he'd have to trust a stranger, he was out of Dillon's reach. The moment of hesitation cost him everything.

Five seconds later, Simon was dragged under

completely. Along with dislodged bushes, branches and stones, he became just one more object bundled down the hill in the avalanche of sediment.

Dillon was kneeling next to his sculpture. Under him, the ground still rumbled like a railway platform when a heavy train thunders past but it still seemed to be secure. On hands and knees, he edged cautiously towards Luke, trying to keep himself safe while getting close enough to help.

Every time Luke pulled his legs out of the water and attempted to scrabble up the bank, more of it gave way, leaving him dangling again. Dillon hung on to another branch and bent down towards Luke's hands and tormented face. Seizing one of Luke's wrists, he began to heave.

Thrashing around with his legs, Luke managed to find a fragile foothold and he shouted, "Get me out of here! Help me!"

Still holding on to the ash with his other arm, Dillon felt as if he were ripping in two. But at least the top of Luke's head was coming up level with solid ground, like a grotesque figure rising from the dead.

Just as Luke got a grip on Dillon's arm with his second hand, disaster struck. The oak trunk of the angry man rushed down with the mud and rammed violently into Luke's stomach like a missile, knocking the wind out of him. He shrieked with pain and let go of Dillon, his last hope. As he slithered under, mud gushing into his mouth, another tree trunk thudded into him. Overwhelmed, he joined the downward stampede.

Further upstream, Cliff lost his slender grip on firm land and was also sinking into the slide. In seconds, he'd be submerged and beyond help. This time, Dillon had a different idea. He scrambled to his feet, tottering on the edge of the crevice. Taking a few steps back from the gully, he grabbed the nylon rope that was still looped over one of the ash's boughs. On his way back, though, he slipped and fell. To save himself from tumbling into the landslide, he put out a hand to grasp the first thing, anything. As his hand slapped down on the unfinished version of Cliff's head, he heard a wretched cry – an awful inhuman noise – from Cliff.

And in the spot where Dillon expected Cliff to be, there was no sign of life. The boy had gone. For Dillon, the shock of falling was replaced by the shock of the malicious earth and the speed of it all. A boy was there at one moment and, in an instant, he'd vanished.

Dillon took his hand away from the sculpture and got to his feet again, frantically scanning the mudslide, looking for any sign of Cliff. For a few seconds, there was nothing but debris. The only things that Dillon recognized were the statues of James Aykroyd and Trooper, the Irish terrier, as they careered past. But then a dark lump appeared midstream. Dripping mud, the bulge became Cliff Aykroyd's face, gasping desperately for breath.

Immediately, Dillon realized why, in the sculpture, Cliff's face looked like a smudged painting. Below him, Cliff's head looked like a waxwork being melted with a flame. As a horror-film effect, it would have been uncomfortable to watch. In the flesh, it was gruesome.

Dillon wrapped one end of the rope around the branch and threw the other end down towards Cliff as the surging swamp swept him along. "Grab it!" he shouted at the top of his voice.

Cliff had taken a mouthful of choking watery sludge. Caked in the stuff, he was terrified, barely able to see. Yet somehow his fingers fumbled for the rope and he hung on.

For Dillon, it was like trying to pull a huge ship up to a quayside by its rope, fighting against a roaring tide. Still trying to make sure he didn't overstep the mark and stumble into the grim deluge himself, he peered over the edge.

His life hanging by a thread, Cliff could do

nothing. He was writhing on the end of the line like an exhausted fish.

All that Dillon could see was Cliff's expression of fright behind a mask of mud. Between gasps for breath, Dillon hauled on the rope, pulling Cliff closer and closer to the bank.

Despite his exhaustion, Dillon clenched his teeth and forced more effort from his aching arms. He yanked on the rope, dragging it little by little over the rough bark, slowly reeling in his catch. Even when Cliff finally reached the edge of the trench, he was far from safe. Dillon had no idea how to lift him out.

Cliff seemed to think he could clamber out of the channel. He let go of the rope and clung instead to tree roots, hoping to use them like the rungs of a ladder. But his sodden clothes were too heavy, his arms and legs too weary, and the roots too slippery. He slumped back in. The fish had got away.

Shattered, Dillon expected to see Cliff plunging

down the side of Bleakhill Top, out of control, partly submerged, just a jumble of arms and legs. But he didn't. Cliff's left foot had caught in a loop of root and tethered him to the spot. Yet, he was lolling helplessly, his head under the gushing water. If Dillon didn't do anything, he'd be drowned in the next minute.

The first branch that Dillon picked up was rotten but he thought that the second would bear Cliff's weight. He lay down, stretching himself out so his shoulders and head were over the edge of the cascade, and thrust the branch downwards, banging it into Cliff's chest so that the boy would know that something solid was within his grasp.

An instinct for life made Cliff clutch at this last straw with his flailing hands.

Once he felt the extra load, Dillon heaved. Right away, Cliff's head rose out of the water, coughing and spluttering – and breathing. As Dillon yanked Cliff up, his foot unhooked from the tree root. When

THE TORTURED WOOD

Cliff got his arms and shoulders onto stable ground, when he'd got a firm grip, he let go of the branch.

Dillon rolled away from the lip and gulped great mouthfuls of air. Cliff clawed himself out of the channel, lurched drunkenly and then crumpled in an untidy heap onto the earth. Neither of them could utter a word.

18

At the edge of Bleakhill Top, Dillon shivered with pleasure. It was March and he was taking his usual short cut to school. Behind him, the sunlit cemetery was vibrant with spring flowers. Before him, parts of the wood had suddenly become carpeted in welcoming green. There were even a few splashes of pale yellow primroses. The footpath was no longer forbidden. A council supervisor had carried out tests and declared the wood safe once more. Apparently, the underground water had been building up for years, but now that it had been released the remaining land was firm and dry.

For the first time this year, Dillon had set out without a coat. Inside the wood, he felt a chill, but it was just a lack of warmth from the sun. Now, the long shadows made Bleakhill Top cool rather than creepy. There was still the noise of running water but it came from a new and picturesque stream that would continually drain water away. Across the brook, someone had put down stepping stones. Further down, where the angry man had once startled Dillon, the bank was adorned with dandelions. Tree roots jutted out from it like handles. Moss and fungus had begun to colonize the fallen trees that had not been swept away.

Suddenly, Dillon caught sight of a movement out of the corner of his eye, and he halted and let out a gasp, his heart thudding for a couple of beats. But then he recognized Alice Burkinshaw as she came towards him, and he smiled. Dillon wasn't the only one who walked through the wood these days. There were often dog walkers and several kids from school.

Alice looked brighter, less scared than when Dillon had last seen her. She said to him, "I saw you in the paper."

Dillon nodded. Alongside *The Eastbridge Journal*'s report of the two deaths in Bleakhill Top, the newspaper had included a picture of Dillon. He'd been described as a local hero for saving Cliff Aykroyd from certain death. His parents had cut out the section on Dillon and put it in the family scrapbook. It was embarrassing but it did prove that his parents were proud of him.

Alice added, "People are still talking about what you did, you know."

"Nothing too bad, I hope."

"Someone said you couldn't have tried hard

enough to save the other two, but that's not what Cliff Aykroyd's saying. He put them right."

Feeling awkward, Dillon looked around and then asked, "No Trooper?"

A look of relief on her face, Alice said, "He's gone. My husband took him. They've both gone. I'm just admiring the wood. New beginnings and all that."

Dillon didn't know what to say. It didn't seem right to congratulate her so he just said, "I see."

"Going to do more carving?" she asked.

Dillon shook his head. "No. I think the place could use a break from that sort of thing. Don't you?"

After the landslide, only Dillon's last piece remained. As for the rest of the carvings, the current of mud had done the council's work. As Dillon walked away from Alice, he glanced down towards the solitary sculpture. He was surprised to see a figure standing there, studying it. Checking his watch, he decided he had time to scramble down as well.

Cliff hardly raised his head. There was an accusation in his voice as he said, "You made it happen, didn't you?"

Dillon did not try to defend himself. "I don't know. Maybe."

"Just like Darius Coe made lightning hit my dad."

"I think so."

Cliff looked up with a stern expression and stared into Dillon's eyes. "Did you mean to?"

"No."

The boy's silence forced an explanation from Dillon.

"It sounds stupid but I didn't know what I was carving. And I didn't know – till near the end – that I'd make it come true. By then, I'd finished Simon and Luke. No going back." He pointed down at the carving. "But I tried to give you hope."

Cliff checked out the scratchy misshapen face again. He hesitated for a few seconds before replying. "You've sure got a funny idea of hope."

Dillon didn't know how to take Cliff's dry comment. It might have been a reprimand but Dillon preferred to think it was a joke.

Quietly, Cliff said, "The band's got a gig coming up at school – in memory of Simon and Luke."

"Yes, I know."

"I don't suppose…"

"What?" Dillon prompted.

"Some of the others think you ought to do a guest appearance or something." Cliff spoke hesitantly, not used to issuing invitations.

Dillon paused before asking, "And what do you think?"

Cliff shrugged. "Not sure. But…I suppose… why not?"

"Okay," Dillon replied with a smile. "It's a deal."

If you have enjoyed

THE
TORTURED
WOOD

you might also like these other
spine-chilling reads...

Kiss of Death
Malcolm Rose

On a school trip to the plague village of Eyam, Seth is moved by the story of how villagers sacrificed their lives to the Black Death. Kim and Wes are more interested in what they see at the bottom of the wishing well – money!

But when they snatch the coins they also pick up something they hadn't bargained for, and as the hideous consequences of their theft catch up with them all, Seth is forced to face a terrifying truth. Has Eyam's plague-ridden past resurfaced to seek revenge?

Past and present collide in this exciting thriller by acclaimed author, Malcolm Rose.

9780746070642

The Lurkers
Charles Butler

"*I may not have much time to write this. The Gates of Memory are shutting all around the town. I've been trying not to think about it, trying not to draw attention to myself, but I have to face the facts. Today, while I still know what the facts are. In a few days I may pick up this notebook and not recognize a word I've written. The Lurkers can do that, you know. I've seen it happen.*"

What are the Lurkers? What do they want? And can Verity stop them?

The Lurkers delves into a nightmare world in the grip of an untouchable enemy.

9780746070659

THE SHADOW GARDEN
ANDREW MATTHEWS

Matty's sixth sense tells her that Tagram House is harbouring a dark secret. The master, Dr. Hobbes, seems charming on the surface but underneath Matty detects a glint of razor-sharp steel. Her fears lead Matty to the eerie Shadow Garden, and she eventually discovers what's buried there. Now she must untangle the mystery before disaster engulfs everyone.

Like cold fingers reaching from the grave, a chilling atmosphere of mystery and suspense seeps through the pages of this haunting ghost story.

"This is a highly atmospheric novel…a satisfying, gripping read with a truly alarming climax."

School Librarian

0 7460 6794 1

SMOKESCREEN
BERNARD ASHLEY

Ellie hates leaving behind her friends, but the worst thing about moving to a pub by the canal is that the dark, swirling waters bring back traumatic memories. And Ellie's troubles only grow when she discovers the shady dealings that take place in the Regent's Arms on Friday nights.

There is somebody who could expose the truth – if only she could escape the evil gang that holds her captive.

Smokescreen is an electrifying thriller that twists and turns through the shadowy underworld of a dangerous trade.

"Gripping stuff." *Publishing News*

0 7460 6791 7

The Curse of Magoria
Paul Stewart

Will anyone escape the deadly dance of time?

According to local legend, Magoria was a powerful sorcerer intent on harnessing time itself. But his experiments went disastrously wrong, and he unlocked a dangerous curse that could strike the mountain village of Oberdorf at any time. When Ryan arrives there on holiday he has no idea that his visit might have deadly consequences...that he might unleash the Curse of Magoria.

A tale of dark magic from the co-author of the hugely successful series *The Edge Chronicles*.

"Mysterious forces are abroad in this nail-biting tale."   *Carousel*

**Winner of the Lancashire School Library
Services Fantastic Book Award**

0 7460 6232 X

The Boy Who Haunted Himself
Terry Deary

There's no escape from the ghost in his mind.

When Peter Stone answers an advert promising to release the hidden power of the mind, he doesn't expect to find anything as squalid as the entrance to Dr. Black's office. And the mysterious doctor isn't quite what he seems either. But Peter is so determined to change his life that he ignores the warning signs...and then it's too late.

Powerless to escape an experiment that goes horribly wrong, Peter finds himself in a life-or-death struggle with an invader in his mind.

A truly creepy ghost story with a difference, from the author of the spectacularly successful *Horrible Histories*.

0 7460 6036 X